Lipstick Clique II

by

David Weaver

To subscribe to

our mailing list,

text TBRS to

22828

SECTION

ONE

She had been on the run for so long that it seemed as though it would never be over. She had been beaten by life on several occasions, but she absolutely *refused* to go down to the canvas. She briskly walked into the supermarket so that she could buy something to eat. Her running had taken her from Pennsylvania to prison, prison to Texas, from Texas to Georgia, from there to Florida; and now she was in the college city of Madison, Wisconsin. Of all of the places that CNN had reported that she could possibly

David Weaver

be, Madison, Wisconsin was definitely not even on their radar.

After the incident in Florida with her former lover, 5; she didn't know what to do with herself anymore. She wasn't angry that he had tried to set her up, she was instead angry that he would try to commit suicide in such a ridiculous manner. That incident had happened over 6 months ago. After the attempted set up, at first she laid low in Florida for a month while working on her new plan. After that month was over, she went on a silent car robbery spree, but not robbing for profit or fun; robbing so that she could slowly make her way to Madison, Wisconsin without being tracked.

After thinking over all of her possible options, that seemed to be the only one that made sense to her.

When she was in prison, she had a friend who worked in the library named Salisha. Salisha had been 34 years old, but had been locked up for 15 years for a manslaughter conviction. She had originally been scheduled to be released after 8 years, but after getting into so much trouble in prison; the Warden decided that the free world would not be the best place for her to participate in at that time. Instead of her paroling out, she had to max out her time.

When Treasure was in Florida trying to figure out if there was anyone in the world that she could even trust for 30 seconds, Salisha came to her mind. She knew Salisha was from Madison, Wisconsin because she was the first and only person that she'd ever met from that place… And Salisha represented her city on a regular basis. In prison, she worked in the library, but only worked there so that she could get the proper material to keep her prison gambling ring running.

Salisha needed access to a copier and printer so she could print the tickets. Plus she needed a "public" place to sit so that the inmates could come put their sports bets in. The day before Treasure broke out, she remembered going to the library to return a book that she knew she would never get a chance to read. When she went to the desk to return the book, Salisha slid the book back to her.

Treasure was confused. "I'm through with the book! Here!"

Salisha looked her in the eyes. "Keep the book! I see things… Make it look better by at least keeping the damn book! Put it in your cell."

David Weaver

Treasure remembered her heart dropping to the floor because her escape could possibly be ruined by some big black lady in the prison library. Worry was evident on her face, and she made no effort to mask it.

"Don't worry Treasure! Take this book, and take your ass up out of here! If it works it works, I'm on your side bitch! Fuck you thought, I was gon' tell the police or something? Please! It's Maddy Wiskey in this bitchhh!"

––––––––––

For the past 5 months Treasure had been in Madison, Wisconsin, waiting on Salisha to be released from prison. Wearing pink lipstick and pink dye in her hair, Treasure looked like a completely different woman. Every day she stalked the local library's computer so she could check Salisha's release status. Treasure was anxious to have a friend out there. She was eager to be around someone that she could at least semi trust... But the day that Salisha was finally released.... All hell broke loose.

"Treasure! I miss you girl! How have you been?" Salisha said as she climbed into the backseat of the cab beside Treasure. "Girl, I saw you all over the damn news! You're just a bad ass out here ain't ya?"

Treasure smiled at Salisha as she stared out of the rear view mirror of the taxi cab. She had too many organizations searching for her and didn't have time to get caught slipping. "Yea I'm a bad ass Salisha. I've been getting some bad-ass sleep, all up in roach hotels sleeping with one eye open and one finger on the trigger. You know this shit ain't right, man tell me you got somewhere safe for me to stay at girl." Treasure said while looking at the cab driver's reflection.

"Excuse me sir… but if you stare at my face one more got damn time…" Treasure spoke softly but firmly. She started thinking about 5 and all of the people who had attempted to remove her from her life. She grabbed her pistol and slid it out slowly, in her own little zone; but Salisha caught her hand.

"Treasure… it's ok baby… put that back up." Salisha said as she looked at Treasure as though she had lost her mind. "You know I just got my

David Weaver

freedom… I'm with you baby, but damn; let me at least go have a damn McDonald's cheeseburger before I go back in."

Salisha smiled as she said those words, but she was dead serious. The only thing she'd had a taste for throughout all of those years in prison was a McDonald's cheeseburger.

"Where to?" The cab driver asked in a rude tone. He had been trying to pay attention to what the girls were saying while in his rear cab, and had found himself becoming more and more irritated.

"To the nearest McDonalds." Treasure said as she brushed off the cab driver and focused her attention back on the vehicles around them on the road. She had it in her mind that she was just absolutely *not* going to prison. She was just absolutely *not* going to end up in a situation where she can be deemed helpless. *Fuck that!*

Salisha bounced up and down in the seat as she stared at the passing scenery. The land was dry and plain, but the most basic of scenery as a free citizen looked like paradise when a person was just exiting the clutches of the prison's grasp. Salisha glanced over at Treasure and grinned. "Baby, let me get some of that pink lipstick. And... gimme a piece."

Treasure reached in her small clutch and grabbed the lipstick. Then she stared at Salisha. "Give you a piece of *what* got damnit!?"

"A piece of *nothing!* Gimme one of those pistols you got! I saw one of them sticking out of your purse- you're such a fucking lady."

Treasure shook her head and frowned. She thought that she'd concealed the other pistol, but perhaps she should have been prepared for a seasoned criminal to be able to point out the fact that it was sticking out. She grabbed her spare pistol and handed it to Salisha. "Now bitch... let me tell you something about this got damned pistol... I have this extra one in my purse because I have to be equipped at all times just in case I run out of bullets. I can't afford for a police officer to put the handcuffs on me. His cuffs belong on his *bitch*."

Salisha burst out laughing. "I guess you don't realize that I'm an old school bitch. You don't gotta tell me the do's and don'ts of this here street shit. Snitching is no-where in my jacket... but this pistol is!" Salisha continued to laugh as she stuck the pistol inside of her denim jacket.

Treasure reached down and grabbed her pink lipstick. Before she handed it over, she sighed. "Listen Salisha... this lipstick is important for me because it's breast cancer awareness month. I bought it in memory of the girl that died in the Welkers Unit in prison. You remember the girl... the young girl who came into the prison with breast cancer- a life sentence on top of a life sentence. When I started hearing about the breast cancer awareness commercials, I just started feeling bad for the ladies going through that. She had lost so much weight, had lost so much of her vitality... I rock this lipstick in order to restore her vital signs."

Salisha closed her eyes as Treasure spoke, absorbed her words and remembered the young girl that she mentioned. It was indeed a sad day in the prison when all of that stuff went down. It was early A.M. breakfast call, and when the cell door locks opened; normally everyone would be on their feet. They couldn't risk being caught off guard in their beds for someone to come through there with a knife and stab them. Hatred was rampant around the prison compound.

"Wake up girl." Treasure said once they arrived at McDonald's. Salisha opened her eyes and stared around at the vehicles in the parking lot. It was certainly a beautiful sight to her. The only time she'd seen the new model vehicles were on television shows and in magazines, so for her to be laying eyes on cars with 24 inch rims were amazing to her.

"Damn Treasure! This is crazy! The last time I was free, small rims that poked out were in style. Big rims like those weren't even out! Man oh man I'm about to enjoy my freedom!" Salisha said with a big grin on her face. Her eyes searched the parking lot like she'd dropped something. She had fallen back in love with life all over again.

The cab driver slowed down and looked in the rear-view mirror. Do you want me to drop you two off here or what?"

Treasure spoke up. "Let's go through the drive through and-"

"Hell nawl!" Salisha screamed. "We are not going through a drive through! I haven't been able to go inside of an establishment freely for too many got damn years now. Fuck that! I wanna go in that muthafucka!"

David Weaver

The cab driver had a skeptical look on his face, and Treasure didn't know what it was for until he spoke on it. "Man…. Look… either somebody has to wait in the car or you will have to pay me for the trip we've taken so far. I can't risk just sitting here and you two disappearing on me."

Treasure continued to look out of the window so that the cab driver wouldn't see her face. She couldn't afford for him to recognize her, it would be the *death* of her! "O.K. I'll wait in the car then. Go ahead Salisha, get you something to eat baby."

Salisha frowned at her. "Nah, I want you with me every step of the way. I don't wanna be around all of those weirdos Treasure. I've only been out of prison for a few minutes now. Walk with me Treasure. Do you have any money to pay him?"

Treasure thought back to all of the money she wasted when she was dealing with her snitch ass ex-boyfriend. She had been forced to leave her money behind after he tried to set her up with the FBI for the million dollar reward. She hated him for that, and knew that one day she would get her revenge; but for now she had to keep living her life the best way she could.

"Yea, I have a few dollars on me Salisha." She reached in her purse thinking she had a roll of cash in there, but didn't see anything. Quickly she flipped her stuff around trying to see if something was covering her money up, and still didn't see it. She opened a zipper compartment thinking the money was in there, and nothing was there either.

"Shit!" Treasure said as she dumped the contents of her purse into her lap. There was no money, but there was a medium sized hole in the corner of her purse. Treasure took her finger and slid her finger through the hole in her purse. She shook her head and lay back against the seat as Salisha stared on. "Salisha, I-"

"Don't worry about it Treasure." Salisha said as she pulled out a few dollars from her pocket. The meter said $27.50, so Salisha was trying to put the right amount together.

"Salisha, I'm telling you... I can just wait in the car. I don't want people staring at me... you know my situation..."

Salisha fanned Treasure. "Don't worry about a thing baby, we got this. Ain't nobody gon do nothing, ain't nobody gon recognize you. Things are going to be fine homegirl."

Treasure took a deep breath as she listened to Salisha talk. Her words sounded good, but she still had reserves because Salisha had been locked up for so long that she didn't have a clue as to what was going on in the real world. She didn't realize how advanced technology had become, or how everyone had cell phones and could call her in with ease. When Salisha got locked up, the only cell phones out were Motorola and Nokia- and now everyone was on smart phones.

"I'm telling you Salisha… I'll wait baby." Treasure said again as she tried to calm her nerves. Even though she looked different, she was still worried that she would be recognized since her face had been on the news for so long.

"Nonsense Treasure! Here nigga… wait on us, we're going to pay you for the second half of the trip when we get out of here." Salisha said as she handed the cab driver the money.

He readily grabbed it and started counting, making sure the money for the first half of the trip was all there. He didn't trust them just because he

David Weaver   16

had picked one of them up from outside of the prison. Then he saw that they had known each other for a while, and that made him not trust either of them. He just had a gut instinct that they were full of trouble.

When he saw that he had the right amount of money, he released the locks on the backdoors of the cab and allowed them to get out. He leaned back in his seat and turned the radio up while he waited on them to handle their business in McDonald's.

He watched them as they went in, looked at the shapes of their bodies and thought that they were definitely in possession of some beautiful physiques. He grabbed himself as he tried to picture them eating each other out- and he smiled as he tried to imagine himself in the middle of a threesome with them. "Damn." He whispered to himself as he watched the pink-haired girl walk in McDonald's.

"Let me order the Angus cheeseburger with bacon on it. I don't want any pickles or onions on it, and please add mayonnaise. Thank you." Salisha said as she placed her order for her food.

David Weaver

She turned and faced Treasure, who had her head pointed down at the floor. "Treasure!" She whispered in a muffled tone. "What do you want to eat? I'll cover it."

Treasure shook her head. "I'm not hungry, I already ate."

Sensing that Treasure was tripping, Salisha leaned over and whispered in her ear. "Baby, stop all of that looking down at the floor; you're making yourself suspicious. Just calm down and act natural. I don't know how in the world you stayed free for this long acting the way you're acting. Calm down."

Treasure sighed and adjusted her black shades as she slowly lifted her head up from the ground. She looked around and noticed that nobody was staring at her. *That's a first.* She thought as she calmed down a bit. Normally there would be people staring at her for whatever reason, and it would always make her paranoid. She knew that she never could tell when someone was out to get her or not. She sighed as she thought about her old friends in the Lipstick Clique, but quickly dismissed any feelings she may have had for them.

They had chosen their routes, and she had chosen hers. She *was* the Lipstick Clique, whether she had someone with her or not. It was her creation, and she would always be herself. Treasure leaned against the rail while waiting on Salisha to fill her large cup up with fruit punch at the soda fountain. Salisha walked back over to where Treasure was standing and had a huge smile on her face.

"Treasure, McDonalds has changed. Now they got free refills and stuff. I can just drink as much soda as I want. I can also mix one soda with the next! That's what's up!"

Treasure stared at Salisha as though she had lost her marbles. She wanted to make a comment, but she thought better about it. She had to let it sink in her mind that Salisha had been locked up for so long that damned near everything was an adventure to her. It was funny in a way, and in other ways it was just sad.

Treasure smiled as she watched Salisha drink out of the cup without having the lid on it. "Lisha, you know the lids are right there… and the straws are back there." Treasure said pointing.

Salisha looked in the direction that Treasure was pointing and fanned her hand. "Oh yea, I already

David Weaver

knew that, I was going to get them when I got over there." She said while trying not to seem so pathetic.

"Order #37!" The lady behind the counter yelled out as she continued to take and process orders.

"That's me!" Salisha said, eagerly walking up to the counter to get her cheeseburger. She took the bag from the lady and pulled the cheeseburger out right there at the counter. She opened the wrapper containing the food and removed the bun so she could see if her order was placed right. It wasn't.

"Aye bitch! You put onions and pickles on this muthafucka! Didn't I tell you I didn't want that shit on my food?" Salisha screamed out, breaking the calm mood that Treasure was in.

The lady behind the counter frowned. "Bitch? Don't be coming in here calling me no bitch! I got your bitch! Bitch!"

Treasure's scalp itched out of nervousness as she listened to the lady behind the counter talk crazy to Salisha. She knew that was not a wise decision; just like her coming into the store with Salisha wasn't a wise decision either. She thought about the situation and decided that she would have to step in before something bad happened. Salisha wasn't out on the run from the FBI like she was, so she had to take extra precaution. Salisha had been released because she had done her time, and she was definitely not about to allow her to ruin her life just because she was pissed.

Treasure walked up to Salisha and was about to tap her on the shoulder, but it was wayyyy too late for that.

Salisha pulled her pistol out of her jacket and jumped on top of the counter. "You said you got my bitch!? Where the fuck is it then bitch?" She screamed as she climbed across the counter and hemmed the girl up in the corner. "Where the fuck is my bitch at? Where is the one you said you had for *me*!?"

Damn. Treasure said as she shook her head. She looked towards the back and saw the manager headed for the telephone and knew that she couldn't allow things to go down like that. *Fuck!* She said as she tried to think of a quick solution. But after all of the thinking she was doing, she only had one solution.

She pulled her pistol out too.

Treasure pointed the pistol in the sky and pulled the trigger. *Wham!* "Everybody get on the muthafuckin' floor! Now!"

She couldn't believe that Salisha had been out of prison not even an hour and she already had her shooting her gun in a public place.

Salisha turned around and stared at Treasure. "What are you doing?"

Treasure stared back at her with a frown on her face. "What the fuck does it look like?"

"It looks like you're robbing them, I'm not trying to rob them; I'm trying to teach this ho a got damn lesson!"

Treasure's lip curled up in disgust at Salisha's response. "A lesson? The only person that's going to get the got damned lesson is your monkey ass. The crime you're committing now is worse than a robbery, and I'm committing the lesser crime by getting us paid."

Treasure slid across the counter and grabbed a stack of McDonald's paper bags out of the holder. She went to the counter and popped it open expertly. She dumped money from the cash register to her paper bags while she watched Salisha punch the girl in the side of the face while hemmed up in the corner. The girl was crying and whimpering, but Salisha didn't give a fuck.

Treasure was concerned at first, until her fingers started brushing across the texture of the hundred dollar bills. To her, there was nothing in this world greater than money; except for a whole bunch of money. She loved it, and ever since she went to prison for her ex-boyfriend, and had been forced to endure prison with no money; she had vowed to always have access to as much of it as she so desired.

If she'd had access to that type of money in the past, then she would have never had that court appointed lawyer; and would have never been offered that bullshit plea deal. She was still angry that the lawyer had gotten away with that, and knew that she would still be angry until she faced her issues head on.

The world seemed to only respect power as a form of payment, and simply being rich wasn't powerful enough. She would have to be rich *and* have a voice in order to be powerful, but she knew that she would need to start some damn where, so she'd start with money.

She raked the money from the cash register and into the bags, and was doing so effortlessly when she came across a register that wouldn't open. She tugged at it and it still wouldn't crack open for her. She frowned and stared for a second when Salisha walked over.

"Aye, what the fuck you doing girl? We're in a fucking robbery! We don't have time for this regret shit that you got going on in your mind. What you gonna do girl? Shit, let's make a move!" Salisha yelled.

"I can't open the motherfucka girl! Do you have any suggestions?"

————

Salisha and Treasure ran out of the McDonalds rapidly. Salisha was glad that she had remained in good shape throughout her prison bid, because otherwise she would never have been able to pull the stunt that she was pulling. She was running behind Treasure and carrying the whole damn cash register.

"Aye bitch, we needa find a car like right now got damnit!" Salisha huffed as she eyed the onlookers who were staring at them in the parking lot. A burst of emotion overtook her as she was instantly reminded of the days before she went to prison. She had been in the streets doing any and everything that produced a profit. She didn't care if she had to rob, kill, sell, or persuade- she was definitely about that life. She had done it all, but the ironic thing was... she had gone to prison for something that she hadn't even done.

Treasure was scanning the parking lot for the easiest vehicle to hotwire, and just like that; her mind went blank. She stood there like a deer in the headlights as she started back thinking about 5 and the betrayal that he lay onto her heart. She stood there panicking as she thought back to Bubbles, and back to the man she had trusted and loved before she went to prison. In a millisecond, everything flashed through her mind. All of the betrayal, all of the hurt and backstabbing and deceit. She gripped her pistol tightly and glanced over at Salisha, who was standing there sweating.

I should just kill her right now because I know she's going to turn on me! Treasure thought as she blanked out.

"Treasure, what's wrong with you bitch? Wake yo' ass up and let's go!" Salisha said as she ran towards a car coming through the drive-through.

"Slide yo ass over! All the way over and out of the got damn car you old motherfucker you!"

Salisha was on beast-mode, and Treasure mentally admonished herself for not trusting her when she knew that she had no reason not to. She was just so sick and tired of being let down in life that it hurt her to even imagine being hurt again. She told herself that she would voice her concerns to Salisha about her emotional scars the first available chance she got. After all, that was the only friend she had left in the world.

She would feel bad to mess up the only friendship she had remaining due to trust issues.

She laughed as she watched the older white man slide across the seat and tumble onto the ground under Salisha's orders. She watched as he ran away in slow motion- although she knew that his slow motion running was more than likely him running at the highest speed he had available. She jumped into the passenger seat and watched as Salisha placed the heavy cash register into the back seat, and then struggle with getting comfortable behind the steering wheel.

Salisha was about two inches short of six feet, and was carrying about 185 pounds of mass on her. She was full figured with an attitude and a pistol. Treasure sighed just thinking about the trouble that they were about to get into together. It had been her objective to just lay low, thinking that Salisha was going to be on some calm and relaxed shit being that she had just done so much time in prison.

What the fuck was I thinking! Treasure thought as Salisha drove the car like it was a bumper car. She bounced off of a pole and kept riding as if nothing had happened. "Damn girl... did you ever have your license before you went to prison? I mean... damn, you just hit a pole and acted like that shit never even happened! What the fuck!"

A car was pulling into the entrance when Salisha was pulling out, and even though there was ample amount of space for both cars to handle their business, Salisha still smashed into the vehicle; causing severe damage.

"Calm yo' ass down Treasure, you're making a bitch nervous as a motherfucker! I was calm as hell robbing McDonald's, but I haven't operated a vehicle in so long that I forgot how this shit works! Just chill and let me get ahold of myself."

"Shit! You want me to drive? I don't wanna be on no high-speed chase with yo' crazy ass if you can't motherfucking drive!" Treasure screamed as she cringed and stared wide-eyed at how Salisha was holding the steering wheel. She had two hands on the wheel and was sweating like she was working out. "Damn girl, it ain't that serious. What the hell is on your mind Salisha?"

Salisha ignored her and ran straight through a red light.

"What the fuckkkk?" Treasure screamed frantically. "Bitch you running red lights like you playing video games and shit! You been reading too many urban fiction books in prison girl. What the fuck is you thinking about? This is the real world!"

Salisha bit down on her lips and hit the brakes too hard while trying to slow down. The car made a brief screeching noise, but she hit the gas to make up for her mistake. "Treasure you making me nervous motherfucker! Calm yo ass down now!"

Treasure sat back and watched in amazement at Salisha's horrid driving conditions. She was panicking, but she was finally able to calm down when Salisha slowed the vehicle and turned down a residential street. The homes on the street were upscale and relaxed, and Treasure felt comfortable because if the police were looking for two armed robbers, it would be the last street they would think of searching at that moment.

She looked around and couldn't imagine who in the hell Salisha could have known who stayed in that area. She started to ask her, but thought better of it. She didn't want things to get worse than they had been with her overly amped up friend. She was just trying to live her life without going back to prison. Treasure did not need the drama.

Luckily, Salisha answered the question before she even had a chance to ask her. "This is my man's house!" she said as she swerved into a driveway going about 30 miles an hour. She smashed on the brakes and the vehicle slid to a screeching halt merely inches away from the house itself.

"I'm convinced you're tryna kill us both Salisha! Damn, slow this damn thing down when you drive. You acting like-"

But before Treasure could even finish her sentence, Salisha was out of the car and running like a mad woman. Treasure couldn't help but to smile at her old friend. For her to have been locked up for so many years and still have somebody to go home to made her feel good. It made her have hope that one day she could have unconditional love such as her friend. It warmed her insides briefly- but they became chilled every time she thought back about 5 and the treachery that he had pulled against her.

She took a deep breath and was about to lay back against the seat when she realized that the car wasn't even in gear. It started rolling backwards and it scared the hell out of her. She jumped over into the driver's seat and held the brakes down long enough to put the car into gear. She shook her head as she watched Salisha bounce off of the toes of her feet in anticipation of seeing her lover.

Treasure surveyed the area, and noticing that it was a calm location; she got out and leaned against the car in an attempt to relax her self. The door burst open and from what Treasure could see, things looked perfect. Salisha's man opened his arms and pulled her into one of the sexiest embraces that Treasure had ever bore witness to. Quickly, Salisha went into his house and the door shut.

Treasure took a deep breath and thought about how good love must feel when it was real. She was so happy for Salisha that she didn't know what to do. It was truly amazing. She went and sat behind the wheel just in case she had to take off if the police came around. It was never a good thing to be in an off-balance position, and she had vowed to never be like that again. She relaxed and waited on her friend to handler her business.

"I miss you so fucking much Nerow! It's been over a decade since we last saw each other, and even to this day, you're still the sexiest and most handsome man I've ever laid eyes on! Damn I love you!"

David Weaver

Nerow blushed as he stood in front of Salisha. He had been doing the entire bid with her- writing her whenever she wrote him, sending her money whenever she asked for it, never missing a birthday or holiday, and just comforting her when nobody else was capable. When she wrote letters to him complaining about her family not being there for her, he replied by telling her that he *was* her family and that she needed nobody else.

"Salisha, I'm just glad that you're finally free baby. I thought those people were never going to let you out of that prison. I'm so happy that you're out. God knows that I couldn't have made it another year without you. If you'd have had to do one more year, I'd have had to break in there and get yo' ass girl!"

Salisha rolled her eyes, knowing that Nerow wasn't about to do shit if she had to do another year. She sat on the sofa and smiled at Nerow while staring him up and down. It had been so long since she'd last had some dick that she wandered if she still knew what to do with it. She licked her lips while staring at Nerow's crotch. She wanted it so bad that she felt a slight trickle of drool start to leak out of the corner of her mouth.

She caught herself quickly. "Well damn... So Nerow... all these letters you've been writing me about what you were going to do to me when I got out of prison... and shit... you haven't done nothing so far. This is a brand new pussy damned near. Ain't no dick been in here in a long ass time. What you gon' do about it? I'm horny as hell."

Nerow stared at her nervously. He took a deep breath, and mumbled something incoherently.

Salisha chuckled at how nervous and humble Nerow was. He had been her ride or die nigga for over 10 years, and a nigga like that just *had* to be saluted. She was going to suck his dick until he bust in her mouth; swallow that shit, spit it back up *and* blow a bubble with it. That nigga had to be treated like a fuckin king for the rest of her life's existence. She thought the world of him.

She walked over to him and rubbed her soft hands across his face. He shuddered on contact, and quickly put his hand up to remove hers.

Salisha was surprised. "What's wrong Nerow? You don't want me to touch you? With all these love letters we've sent each other you should be good and ready by now!"

David Weaver

Nerow stood up instantly and backed up a couple of feet.

"What the hell is wrong with you Nerow?" Salisha asked in a quiet and confused tone.

Nerow stared back at her without speaking. He crossed his arms and took a deep breath. His reading glasses rose up and down on his nose with each deep breath he took. "Salisha... it's just that it's been so long... You know... I kinda feel like I don't know you at all anymore. It's like... you're a stranger."

Salisha was pissed. "What the fuck you mean I'm a got damn *stranger?* All the time I did in prison was time that I did *for you!* What happened to us being together Nerow? What was all this shit you sent me in these letters? I thought you wanted to be with me?"

Nerow started to answer, but his eyes immediately went towards the front door; where a key was being worked into a lock. Suddenly the door opened.

"Nerow baby! I'm home!" A light skinned woman with jet black shoulder length hair screamed as she walked into the house. Her stilettos smacked the surface of the floor with so much vigor and importance that it was no way that she could be mistaken for anything other than the woman of the household.

A little girl ran through the house full speed ahead until she had her arms around Nerow's leg. "Daddy! Can I go on the field trip tomorrow?"

Daddy? What the fuck? Salisha thought to herself as she stared at Nerow's spitting image. The little girl looked identical to him, so there was truly no mistaking that it was his child. Salisha felt her world crash right before her very face. She was so hurt that she didn't know what to do.

"Salisha, I can explain. I-"

"How old is your daughter?" Salisha interrupted as she stared at the little happy girl.

She watched as Nerow's eyes lit up when he was talking about his daughter, and it rocked her to her core. She had always known that she would never be in a position to have a child, and that was her main worry about Nerow always claiming that he was going to wait for her. She knew that he wanted a family of his own, and by her being unable to provide him with one, it always made her insecure.

Time and time again, Salisha had constantly begged Nerow to move on with his life. She had cried on the phone on numerous occasions about her plight. She figured that by the time she got out of prison, the gift of motherhood that every woman possessed- would have escaped her. And she cried herself to sleep on many nights when she thought about how loyal of a man Nerow was to sacrifice his fatherhood- simply because the government had stripped her of her motherhood.

Nerow placed his hand on his little girl's head and smiled at her. Salisha stared at the picture in a trance, as if there was no way in the world that that could possibly be happening to her. Her man- the man who had told her that he was going to be with her forever and wait on her no matter how long it took, had started a family of his own without her.

"Salisha…. This is Lisha. She's six years old."

Just as Nerow was finishing his statement, the lady of the house walked over and cleared her throat.

"Hey baby, who's your little friend here?" The lady asked as she stared at Salisha's cheap prison release attire. Looking at the woman of the house made Salisha even more insecure about her own paltry looks. Her hair wasn't anywhere near the caliber of the lady of the house, and her hygiene was about ten years away from being up to par with hers.

Nerow started stuttering trying to get his thoughts out, and Salisha suddenly felt bad for him. After all, he held her down when nobody else did- even though he ended up lying about things in the end. She was confused about it all and had no idea on how to proceed. Instead, she did what she thought was the right thing.

"My name is Salisha. I'm an old friend of Nerow's. I just moved back into the city and I was just coming by to say hello to you all." Salisha said as she started searching for the clearest path to the exit.

"Well, my name is Jamiya. I'm Nerow's wife of 8 years. It's nice to meet you Salisha." The lady of the house said as she stared holes into Salisha.

Salisha felt like she was in the twilight zone. Her brain was scrambled and she could barely believe her

David Weaver

ears. She couldn't believe it. Nerow had tricked her into believing that he was waiting on her all along, when in reality; he never thought that she would ever get out of prison. In all of her years, she could never remember feeling as sad as she felt at that very moment. The man she had loved had crushed her to her core.

"Are you feeling sick Ms. Salisha?" The little girl asked as she stared into her face closely.

Unable to utter another sound, and too choked up to stand in front of them without crying; she turned and swiftly walked out of the house. She felt like the biggest fool in the world for having the thoughts that she'd possessed. Once the door closed, she stood on the porch and took a deep breath. She glanced at the car and remembered that Treasure was still out there waiting on her, and that she couldn't allow her to see her in that situation.

She quickly got her story together and made her way to the car.

"Hey Salisha!" Treasure said as she smiled at her. Salisha's tone had visibly changed from the excited and happy woman she had been before she went inside the house, but Treasure couldn't tell if the change of spirit was because of her being overly emotional, or if something bad had happened.

Treasure started the car up and watched as Salisha wiggled herself into the front seat. No matter how wild Salisha was, Treasure really cared about her friend. She was the only true friend she had left.

"Hey Treasure! I'm crazy excited right now. My man couldn't keep his hands off me. As soon as I got in the house he was hard as a fuckin' rock! I was like damn baby, I know you want it; hell, I want it too!" She lied smoothly.

Treasure grinned at her. "So why the hell you come back out to the car? You know I can handle myself! And who was that lady that came in there? She didn't run you off did she?"

Salisha laughed it off. "Treasure, I got a spot you can stay in until you find a better situation. As a friend, I respect you more than to leave you out here while I'm in the house with my legs up in the air. I'll take you over there and let you get comfortable, then I'ma' come back and get this werk!"

Treasure smiled and put her seatbelt on. "O.K. Salisha, that's good. I'm so happy for you. You're a real friend and if anyone deserves happiness, it's you!" She noticed that Salisha ignored her question, but decided not to force anything out of her only friend.

Salisha smiled and exhaled. She knew she deserved happiness, at least she *felt* as if she deserved it; but it seemed as though life had other plans laid aside for her and only her. "O.K. let's back up and go down this street. The place is like ten minutes away."

It was a small subdivision with perfectly manicured lawns, and exquisitely built homes. "Hold on one second Treasure, let me check something out real quick. Pull up to that house that says 4-17."

Treasure did as she was told, and watched as Salisha got out of the car and walk up to the house. She watched as Salisha went under the doormat and pulled a key out from under there. She opened the door and walked in.

A few minutes later, she walked out and briskly went back to the car. "O.K. everything is set up

Treasure. Here's the key." She said as she stood at
Treasure's window with one hand on her hip.

"Is everything ok Salisha?" Treasure asked her. It
seemed as though Salisha's mood and vibe had
altered and had only gotten worse, but Treasure
couldn't really pinpoint it or the reason if there was
one.

"Everything is fine Treasure. I'm just horny as
hell! I need you to get out of my car so that—"

"Your car?" Treasure asked as she eyed her
suspiciously. She was serious but had a playful
demeanor when she asked.

"I'm joking. *Our* car of course… We both put in
the work for it… But I really need to use it baby girl.
I just wanna go spend some time with my man if
that's ok."

Treasure smiled as she grabbed a couple of the
bags of money. "You know I was joking Salisha. Go
catch up on life. I'll see you in a couple of days.
There should be plenty of money in those McDonalds
bags- there should be enough so that you can get
yourself together. You need your hair done, nails
done, a facial, a wardrobe… You just need to get out

David Weaver

there and become a woman again baby. Do that for me ok?"

Salisha hugged her friend as soon as she stood up. "I will Treasure. Thank you so much for being a true friend to me. No matter how bad people have let me down, one person I know that I can count on is you. And I thank you so much."

Treasure looked out the window as Salisha backed the car up until she'd ran over a mailbox.

Damn that bitch can't drive. I hope she parks that car soon though, that shit's stolen. She's tripping.

Treasure sat down on the sofa and placed her forehead in her palms. She thought about her life before prison, her life during prison; and her life after prison. All she wanted at that point in life was some stability, and someone to really love her.

She had gotten a taste of real love when she was dealing with 5, but it had turned out to be not as genuine as she thought it to be. Just having a *taste* of real love was only enough to whet her appetite. She was longing for a man's touch, yearning for the touch of a gentleman; but at the same time, she didn't want to become betrayed again. She thought about 5 and all of the good times they'd had together. She wondered where his snitching ass was, and if he knew that he was a marked man.

She emptied the money out of the bag and started counting it. To her surprise, the money in the McDonald's bag was comprised mainly of 1's, 5's, 10's, and a few 20's. She counted up to $580 and sighed.

Well damn! I guess it's going to be time to go to work soon.

She turned on her favorite hobby- the news, and sat there absorbing everything that CNN had to say. She knew that it was only a matter of time before they announced a Treasure sighting in Wisconsin, and when she heard it; she wanted to be able to prepare herself for it in advance.

Salisha parked around the corner and waited in the bushes on Nerow's family to leave the house. She

David Weaver

was confused because everything that she'd asked Nerow to do for her, he did it. For all of those years, he maintained the house that her Grandmother had passed down to her- and the same house, she had been able to put one of her best friends up in it so that she could lay low. She was proud for that, but she was sad because she didn't really have anywhere to stay.

But after living with women for so long, she couldn't imagine crowding Treasure's space like that. She would go to a shelter if it came down to it. She was loyal to a fault, and there was nothing that could stop her from being that way.

As soon as the lady of the house and his daughter got into their car, she started making her way out of the wet bushes and on her way to the house. There were a few things that she needed to address, and there was no better time than the current moment.

She knocked on the door and waited patiently. She listened as she heard the sound of Nerow's feet make an audio trail through the house and up to the door. She heard nothing for a second, then she heard the door lock unlatch. The door opened and Nerow stood before her staring.

She tried to walk in, but he didn't budge.

"Nerow! I need to talk to you!" Salisha said angrily. She couldn't believe he was acting that way, and she desperately wanted some answers.

"We have nothing to talk about Salisha. I looked out for you throughout your bid. I did everything you asked me to do, plus I gave you a fantasy life so that you wouldn't be lonely while behind those bars. I had to live my life, and that's exactly what I've been doing."

Salisha felt her heart drop to the floor as she stood there realizing that she had been living a lie the entire prison bid. "Damn you Nerow! You made me fall deeper in love with you and then you just leave me hanging? That's some bullshit! Especially after I did this entire prison bid for *you*!"

Nerow turned his face away trying to avoid looking at her, but she reached in and grabbed his face. "No, look at me Nerow. Look at my face. I gave away everything that life had to offer all because I loved and still love you. I gave away my right to childhood because I took the charge of a crime that *you committed. You* robbed and shot those white people that night Nerow, and dropped the gun off at my apartment.

"They saw you coming out of my apartment, arrested you; and searched my apartment- and that's where they found the weapon. I was under the impression that you'd only robbed them, not *robbed and shot* them; otherwise I would have never told them that I was the person responsible for it. I put myself in prison because I didn't want to see you go to prison. So when I found out that you'd *shot* the victims also, I was naturally pissed Nerow.

"I was pissed off for over a decade. I can't believe you did that to me and—"

"Well what the fuck do you want from me Salisha? It wasn't like you were a saint! You were robbing, killing, stealing, wheeling, and dealing your damn self! You weren't walking around with a halo on your head. And furthermore, the crime I did was nothing *close* to the extreme crimes that you did yourself!"

"Yea, but it's a fucking difference Nerow! The difference is that I didn't get *caught* for the shit I did! I got locked up on some muthafucking *bullshit* Nerow!"

"Salisha really? I did everything for you! I'm broke from dealing with you. Every time you told me to jump, I jumped; even if my finances were fucked up." Nerow said to her while standing there trembling.

Salisha could tell that he was sincere, and in all actuality Nerow had done nothing wrong to her. He had been perfect, and she was just upset that she couldn't have him now that she was home. She would have to respect him for everything that he had done in the past and move on to the present day.

"You're right Nerow. I... You... I..." Salisha was so lost that she couldn't even figure out how to begin her sentence. She was choked up and amazed that Nerow had done the things that he'd done to her. She was confused, and didn't know if the stuff he'd done was good or bad. She could no longer think straight, and it just felt like her entire life had been snatched away from her in one moment.

"I... umm... well, Nerow I just wanted to bring you your money back. I have it right here in these McDonald's bags." Salisha said as she awkwardly handed him the bags of stolen money.

"No Salisha. That's your money and I want you to keep it. The things that I have done for you were done because of the things you have done for me. And as far as I'm concerned, you don't owe me shit. Now I may be a little wrong on my end for leading you on, but I damn sure was there for your ass wasn't I?"

Tears slowly started welling up in her eyes as she looked at the man that she had dreamed about for all of those years. She had fallen deeper in love with him as the days went by, and could never have imagined that everything he had been telling her was just to make her time go by better.

She thrust the bags of money in his hands and hurriedly turned to leave.

"Salisha take your money!" Nerow yelled out after her. But she was a woman on a mission. She just wanted to repay him for his troubles and move on with her life. She cried because she loved him deeply enough to shed tears, and she hurt because she'd fallen in love with the man in the love letters; and outside the envelope that man didn't exist.

She rounded the bend and saw a police officer looking into the stolen vehicle that she'd been riding in. She automatically turned and walked in the opposite direction. A deep sense of dread ran through her body as she thought about the consequences of getting caught with a stolen car.

She hadn't been out of prison a whole 12 hours yet, and was already doing some of the craziest stuff that she could think of. *I'll have to just lay low for a while*, she thought as put some pep in her step. She knew that she couldn't go back to where Treasure was staying at because that would be too embarrassing.

She knew that staying with Nerow was out of the question, and when she thought about her situation; she wished that she would have held on to the money until she got in a better position. She was dead broke with only about $35 to her name. She felt like she couldn't waste that $35 of hers on a cheap hotel room, it was pointless. The only option she could come up with was sad, but necessary. She was loyal to Treasure and respectful of Nerow, even after she felt deep down inside that he had done her wrong.

She spit onto the cement as she made a left turn through a backstreet. She cut between a few houses and went down an old path that led her to come out on a main street. She was depressed; but she knew that soon she would be over her problems. Experience had taught her that time healed all wounds, no matter how big the puncture, no matter how small the cut.

There was a long line of people standing outside of an old abandoned warehouse. They were mainly women, mostly drug addicts; and they all seemed to have had a hard life. *I'm no better than them. Fuck it, I'll stay here until I get my life together.*

She got into the back of the line and waited patiently to see if she could be accepted into the shelter for the homeless.

———————

Jamiya came home and immediately went into the kitchen to start the evening's meal. She loved to cook and clean, and did both activities without being asked. She was an old fashioned woman who believed that if she didn't cook for Nerow, there was a high chance that he would find a woman who would fill her shoes.

She had pulled the chicken out earlier that morning, and was about to start cleaning it when she heard a loud commotion in the other room. The noise startled her at first, but when she heard somebody yelling, she knew there was a problem. She immediately walked towards the direction of the ruckus, genuinely concerned about her husband.

But when she walked out of her kitchen and saw two police officers holding Nerow down, she didn't know what the hell to do anymore. "What's happening Nerow?" Jamiya grunted in a choked up voice. The look on her face showed a level of disgust that Nerow had never seen before.

"It's a misunderstanding baby!" Nerow screamed as he wiggled and tried to force the issue with the officers.

Jamiya stood there with her mouth agape, a knife in one hand and a piece of raw chicken in the other. She stared at her husband and a feeling of rage went through her body as she saw him being transported out of the house. Nerow had been everything to her, a comforter and a lover; a best friend and husband- he had been the man who had shown her that every black man wasn't the same, and in one day he had become a statistic.

"Don't wait up ma'am, he's not coming home anytime soon. He's going in for assisting with an armed robbery." The officer said nonchalantly.

Robbery? The reason it hurt Jamiya the most was because in the beginning of their relationship, Nerow had informed her of how he got down in his past; but had insisted that he had changed his old ways.

"Nigga you back robbing? You think I'm gon' wait five to ten years? You think I'm going to be out here struggling as a single parent while your ass is living free in a prison cell off of tax payer's dollars? Nigga you got me fucked up severely."

Nerow couldn't believe his wife was coming at him like that, and it hurt him to hear those words come from her mouth. He had done everything in his power to take care of his wife and child, and ensure that they never had to want for anything. He worked two jobs when he had to, was dedicated and loyal; and never cheated on his wife. He had been what he thought was the ideal husband, a rare breed.

"Jamiya, I'm telling you it's a misunderstanding! Can't you just have a little patience while everything is sorted out?" Nerow begged as the officer led him through the front door and onto the porch.

The other officer turned and held up the McDonald's bag and showed her the money that was inside it. She instantly clasped her hands around her mouth in shock and shook her head in disbelief. "Yea, I don't think he's going to be coming home anytime soon."

Jamiya flopped back against the sofa once the officers were gone and Nerow was hauled off in a police car. She closed her eyes and thought about the possibility of her being loyal and waiting on Nerow to do a prison bid. She wanted to be able to do it, but in her heart she just knew that she wasn't the person to be a dedicated prison wife. She wanted to either be attached or be searching for an attachment.

She drifted off to sleep with several heavy thoughts on her mind.

———————

David Weaver

"Ma'am you would have to sign up in advance to stay at the Rhyland Center. You can't just walk in. I'm sorry. Would you like to sign up to stay here tomorrow?"

Salisha frowned at the lady holding the clipboard. "Tomorrow? But I'm fuckin homeless today bitch!"

The lady's facial expression changed. "O.K. what's your name?"

"Salisha McMann."

"OK. Salisha McMann… I'm writing your name down right now. I'm letting them know that you have been forever banned from staying here. Go stay in the streets with the rest of the fuckin drug addicts you slut."

Salisha had the right mind to swing on the lady, but instead; she said fuck it and turned to leave. She didn't know of any place in the world she could stay, so she decided to go back to her old stomping grounds. She really didn't want to do that because she knew that she would only end up doing the same things that she was doing in her past. She felt like she was too old to keep up with that lifestyle, but it looked as though life was giving her no other choice.

Treasure had dozed off when the doorbell sounded. She jumped up at the sound of it, angry at herself for being so comfortable at a place she knew nothing about. She figured it was Salisha at the door, so she made her way to go open it for her.

But when she got to the window, she almost pissed on herself. There was a police car out front and two officers were standing at the door. She scanned the room quickly, looking for a hiding place in case they decided to burst in.

Damn, I know Salisha didn't just set me the fuck up! Wow! Treasure thought as she ran back to the table and retrieved her pistol. She made her way back to the door and closed her eyes for a second. She had committed so many murders that two more officers wasn't going to bother her, however; she knew that if she wanted a peace of mind that those two more officers needed to stay alive. But she'd rather they die than her. She put a bullet in the chamber and prepared to open the door and shoot both of them but stopped when she heard one of them speak.

"Yea, our snitch said this is where we could find Salisha. Maybe she's not back yet. We'll have to come back later."

Treasure peeped through the window as the officers walked off and back to their patrol cars.

Damn! Somebody is already snitching on Salisha? Her ass has been out only a few fuckin hours! Shit! I gotta go get my girl!

Salisha passed the blunt back to Mazzy as she sat on the back porch relaxing. Mazzy had been an old friend of Salisha's, but had hurt Salisha's feelings when she told her that she had been retired from the robbery lifestyle. Salisha sat there and stared at the beautiful backyard that life had given to Mazzy.

"You have a nice life Mazzy. A really nice one."

Mazzy finished the blunt and sat back in her seat. "Thank you Salisha."

Salisha closed her eyes and enjoyed the calm environment while she could. She was in a deep trance when the phone rang. Mazzy jumped up and ran to it as if her life depended on it.

Salisha noticed how quick she made it to that phone, but decided not to bring the subject up. It wasn't that important. She closed her eyes again.

"Salisha, wake up girl!" Mazzy said as she stood in front of her nervously.

She opened her eyes and stared at Mazzy with a dumbfounded look on her face. "I'm awake! What the fuck is the problem?"

"OK listen! My husband is a detective at the precinct. That's why I quit the game, because I fell in love with the man who was investigating me. Right now we're partners on a lot of shit, but it's still a lot of shit I keep from him involving these streets. Basically, I'm like the most valuable bitch in the streets right now because I can keep people from going to prison and a whole bunch of other shit.

He just called and said to keep my ear to the streets for a bitch named Salisha! He said that they arrested somebody and they implicated you in a robbery! I don't know what to tell you except you better get the fuck away from my house immediately!"

Wow! Treasure set me up! Salisha thought as she stood up from the chair. "Well, where the fuck am I going to go Mazzy? I don't have anybody to stay with at all! I'm just lost in the damn world. I'm out here by myself! I'm fucked up man. I'm all the way fucked up. Please help me. I know you know somebody!"

Mazzy took a deep breath and thought for a moment. "OK, I have somewhere for you to stay. I have someone who will take great care of you, but I'm telling you right now it's going to cost you big time. These people have me on their payroll to help them get away with robberies and shit. They-"

Salisha burst out laughing. "Bitch you still the same bitch! You ain't never changed! You still fuckin with the streets, but you just getting over on bitches now instead of getting your fuckin hands dirty! You-"

"Bitch do you want the plug or what? I don't need my life discussed. I know what the fuck I'm about. If you're going to fuck with them, you're going to pay me. If you're not going to fuck with them, then... I'll have to help my husband out and turn you in."

Angrily, Salisha reached down to pull her pistol out and discovered that it was gone. "What the—"

"Looking for this?" Mazzy said as she held the pistol up for Salisha to see. "I been took this shit off of you when you first dozed off! Bitch you need to wake your ass up if you expect to survive out here in these streets. Shit done changed since you last roamed this bitch!"

Salisha sighed, her heart beating three times its normal rate and sweat collecting on her forehead. She couldn't believe she had done and survived all of that prison time and was still out there in the streets slipping like a rookie. She knew she had to step her game back up if she was going to survive.

"Fine Mazzy! Who the fuck are these people? How do I meet them?"

Mazzy smiled a sinister smile. She knew was going to have Salisha eating out of the palms of her hand, and she couldn't wait to collect the profits from the robberies she was about to be on.

"They're called the Crazy White Boys. Here, take this cell phone and I'll have them meet you somewhere. It's your job to lay low until you get with them though, and from that point on; they're going to take good care of you."

"White boys? You got me fucked up! I ain't fuckin with no-"

"What choice do you got? Either you get with the fuckin program or find you a program to get with in prison!"

Salisha shook her head angrily. She reached out and snatched the cell phone from Mazzy. She took a deep breath and turned to walk off. She stopped in her tracks, and without turning around she asked "What about my gun? Do I get it back?"

Mazzy ran over, lifted her right foot and kicked Salisha off the porch. "You ain't getting shit! Go meet up with my folks bitch! I run this shit!"

Salisha fell down the steps and ended up busting her lip on the ground. She couldn't believe her old friend was doing her like that, but she knew that at some point she had to realize that nobody in life was to be trusted.

Mazzy stood over here with her pistol pointed in Salisha's face. "Am I fuckin' clear yet bitch? I run this shit! You do what the fuck I say do and don't worry about the small shit. Get the fuck out of here!"

Mazzy smiled as she watched Salisha's big ass get up and walk off swiftly. She laughed once she was gone and sat down on the porch talking to herself.

"Damn that bitch is fast. She ran like a track star! Fuckin bitch! Get me my money ho! Hahahaha!"

"Please let me go officer! I told you everything I knew about the robbery, which isn't much. I also told you everything I knew about Salisha! Please let me go because I am of no benefit to you locked up behind bars. Let me get in the streets and get you some more information. Please." Nerow begged as his tears fell to the table. He didn't want his wife to leave him and was willing to do anything to prevent that, including wear a wire if he had to.

The two police officers glanced at each other knowingly. The first officer walked over and patted

David Weaver

Nerow on the back gently. "Nerow I know you've told us everything you know. Unfortunately everything you know just isn't enough to let you walk away without doing some time."

When Nerow looked up, the officer knew he had him. Nerow had the look of a frightened child who was about to be punished, and his teeth were rattling in fright. "Please officer! Please! I'll do anything!"

The officer looked at his partner. His partner nodded his head and walked out of the room.

Nerow walked out of the police station full of anger. He had changed his life for his wife, and at the first sign of danger; she had turned on him. He hated her for that. He had worked diligently to suppress the old Nerow so that he could be a great father and husband, and his wife had thrown it all out the window like it was nothing. He was pissed.

The officer pulled around in a white Dodge Challenger and got out. Nerow looked around to ensure that nobody was looking, then he went and got inside of the vehicle. He drove off thinking about everything the officers had asked him to do. He laughed to himself as he drove the brand new car. He laughed because he knew that he wasn't going to do any of the things the officers had asked.

He was simply trying to escape the clutches of the law by doing whatever he could. He knew exactly what he was about to do, and there was nothing that anyone could do to change his mind about it.

Treasure checked to make sure that the coast was clear, and then she slipped out of Salisha's house under the cover of the dark. She had to go find her friend so that she could help her get the fuck away from those snitches, whoever they were. For someone to have told so fast, she figured that it had to be the dude she was fucking with. But then again, she thought that maybe it wasn't him since he had rode the entire bid out with her. *He has no reason to tell.* Treasure thought as she walked briskly down the street.

By the time she got to the corner of the street, she saw a light shining behind her from a car. She ignored it and kept walking, until the car got right beside her. When she saw that the car was a police car, she almost fainted. There was only one officer in the car and he was driving along at the same pace that she was walking. "Hey, did you just come out of that house?" He asked, on deaf ears.

Treasure kept walking as if he'd said nothing.

Until he jumped out of the car. Treasure wasted no time. She turned and fired. *Wham! Wham! Wham!* Three bullets made him hit the ground like raindrops. She took off running into the shadows of the night. She didn't know where to go, but she knew that she would have to get the fuck out of Madison, Wisconsin as soon as she spoke to Salisha. She was well aware that the police cars had camera systems on them, and that her activities would be well documented on breaking news in the near future.

She ran until she made it to the block where Salisha's boyfriend lived, and ran to the house and knocked on the door. She was sweating and scanning the block in a paranoid state of mind. She knocked on the door again, this time harder; and waited as patiently as she could. When there was no answer after a few seconds, she turned to leave.

Halfway down the steps, a door opened and shut quickly. Treasure turned around and saw the lady from earlier standing there with her hands on her hips. "Who the fuck are you?" She asked Treasure with an attitude.

"What? Naw bitch, who the fuck are you? I'm looking for Salisha."

"Salisha's ass don't motherfucking live here bitch! I live here! You and Salisha done got my husband sent to prison for who knows how motherfucking long and you got the nerve to show up at my fuckin house—"

It was like a thousand lightning bolts hit Treasure all at once. Right away she knew who the snitch was, and she had to go do something about it before shit got any thicker than it already was. She turned and started running back into the darkness.

About two blocks over, she saw a house with all of the lights off as if they were sleep; and there was an older model Honda Accord sitting outside, just ready for the taking. She picked up a rock and bust the window on it. She stuck her hand threw the window, popped the lock, and opened the door. She hotwired the car and left the street.

So that she wouldn't stick out like a sore thumb, she let both of the front windows down in the car. She didn't want someone wondering why the hell she was riding around with a hole in her window. There was too much on the line. She looked at the gas gauge and saw that the gauge was almost on E.

Fuck. How the fuck you park a car that has no gas in it? She asked silently.

She reached for the money in her purse and just like before… it had fallen out of the small hole in her bag. *Fuck! I know what I'ma have to do. Damnit man!*

———

Salisha stood outside of a convenience store waiting on the Crazy White Boys to call her so that she could get the fuck off the streets. She had been standing there for an hour straight waiting on them to call her cell phone. She checked it again to make sure that the phone was indeed turned on. When she saw that it was, she exhaled and shook her head.

A white Challenger slowed down when it drove by the store, and Salisha immediately started looking for an escape route. *I'm not getting bagged by no undercover cops and shit!* She thought as she turned and started crossing the street at a frantic pace.

It seemed that the car was indeed following her. When she crossed the street, the car crossed the street also. When the car slammed on breaks and the door opened, she was about to take off running.

"Salisha, it's me!"

She stared at Nerow like he was the scum of the earth. "What the fuck you want with a bitch like me? I don't need no more fuckin fantasies Nerow! Go and be with your fuckin family you bitch made nigga!" She screamed.

She was surprised that she was holding on to so much emotion and anger, but she was elated that she was able to finally release it.

"I'm sorry Salisha! I love you baby! I don't want nobody else in this world but you. I fucked up bad thinking you were never coming home. I swear to God I'm sorry baby!"

Confused, Salisha walked towards him ready to punch him in the face. "What the *fuck* are you talking about Nerow? You're a married man! You're a

David Weaver

fucking family man! A father! Stop trying to play fuckin games with me you fucking bastard!"

"I love you Salisha!"

"Fuck you Nerow!" She screamed. She wanted to haul off and swing on him but she couldn't. She wanted to spit in his face but couldn't force herself to have the energy.

Instead she sighed, and turned to leave; but Nerow grabbed her arm. She stood still as the touch from his hand to her skin sent electric tingles from the top of her head to the bottom of her feet.

"I said I love you, Salisha!"

Nerow turned her around and gave her a passionate tongue kiss. The power of the kiss started to tear away at Salisha's wall. She was supposed to hate Nerow, not falling for his tricks. She was supposed to hate Nerow because of the way he had betrayed her. She was angry for still loving him. She was angry at the faults that women were born with; the faults of loving someone who didn't truly love them back.

"I love you too Nerow but you're confusing the fuck out of me. Please stop hurting me!" Salisha screamed as tears streamed down her face. It had been so long since she shed tears that she thought she was bleeding. She grabbed at her face out of embarrassment, and when she realized that they were only tears; she became even more embarrassed.

"Come with me Salisha. I can explain everything baby. Come with me please."

Salisha started walking towards the white Dodge Challenger when her cell phone rang and scared her. She stopped and picked the phone up. The phone was ringing and vibrating and she was trying to figure out how to answer it. Embarrassed for her, Nerow hit the *answer* button for her. Salisha looked at Nerow with a confused look on her face.

Nerow motioned to her to put the phone up to her face and speak.

"Hello?"

"Yea, this the Crazy White Boys, so where you at?"

What the fuck? Salisha thought to herself. *No hello? No how are you doing? These motherfuckers, I swear!*

David Weaver

"Man… why do y'all sound like women? I thought—"

"Ain't no time for questions bitch I said this the Crazy White Boys, where the fuck you at?"

Salisha took a deep breath and thought about her options. Her old friend had gotten caught and turned into a snitch, so there was no way she was about to go that route. She had to work for Mazzy to remain free.

"Shit I'm over at the store by the Inn Town Suite hotel. Hello? Helllooo?" Salisha pulled the phone from her ear with a dumbfounded expression on her face.

"Is everything ok?" Nerow asked?

"Yea I'm good. Look Nerow, let me get up with you later. I got some business I need to tend to."

Nerow shook his head. "Listen Salisha. I'm getting the fuck out of the city in about three days, so either you're going to roll with me or not. I'm storing my number into your cell phone and saving it under speed dial. So when you need me, just hold down the number 7 ok?"

Salisha nodded her head as she stared at the man she knew she would love forever. She knew she would be using that number as soon as she handled whatever little business she had with the Crazy White Boys. She knew that Mazzy was trying to use her and come up on a lick, but at the same time she knew that she needed some money of her own. She couldn't survive holding on to that same $35 forever.

"Ok Nerow." Salisha said as she watched him go back and get into his white Challenger. She loved that man so much.

Treasure pulled into the Krispy Kreme drive through and placed an order for a dozen glazed donuts. She waited patiently in line until it was her turn to pay at the window. The lady wearing the hat and the headset smiled at her and leaned out of her window slightly.

"One dozen glazed donuts. That's $7.30."

Treasure went in her pocket with her left hand and balled it into a fist. She stretched her fist out towards the lady's hand, and when the lady placed

David Weaver

her hand under Treasure's; Treasure grabbed her hand forcefully. The lady pulled back, but Treasure had a pistol pointed at her with her right hand.

"Dump them donuts out and fill my shit with cash. And bitch I swear you only got 60 seconds before I start putting holes in more shit than donuts!"

Frantically the lady dumped the pastry products and started emptying the cash register for Treasure's benefit. The gas light came on in the car and Treasure started to panic. After about 20 seconds she screamed out. "Gimme the fucking box!"

She grabbed the box and pressed the pedal down to the max. She couldn't get far because she was afraid the car was going to run out in the middle of a high-speed chase. Her original plan was to rob the donut place for money and pay for gas, but it seemed like she was going to have to go straight to plan two.

She stopped at the first store she saw and scanned the gas pumps. The only thing available was an RV truck, and although Treasure didn't know if she would be able to drive it safely; she knew that she would have no other option other than to try to drive that big shit. That car she was driving was too hot to even attempt. She started making her way to the RV, and before she even got within thirty feet; the engine started up and the white guy pumping the gas stopped abruptly. He replaced the pump while staring at Treasure like she was a lunatic. He hurriedly opened the door, jumped in and slammed it.

Damn, do I look that bad or something? Treasure thought as she watched the RV take off. She looked around desperately, but saw nobody in sight that she could possibly use to help her out of her situation. As a last resort, she ran into the store so that she could pay for gas in the stolen car and froze as soon as she made it to the counter. There were two televisions hanging on the wall and both of them were on different channels.

Although on different channels, both of them said the exact same thing. *Breaking News!*

Treasure stared at her face on both television screens and panicked as she tried to concentrate on both sets of voices at the same time. *"Authorities say they will be actively seeking the death penalty! She is armed and dangerous, and if you see her; call 911 after the sighting. Authorities say she is responsible for a variety of murders all over the country! She has been able to elude authorities for quite some time,*

and has been laughing in the face of the government!
She is a prison escapee-"

The girl behind the counter was staring at the television screens transfixed until she saw Treasure staring at her.

"Holy shit! It's you!"

Treasure pulled her gun out, unsure of whether to kill her in the store; or to rob her and leave another witness.

"You're so fuckin cool Treasure! I follow your shit like everyday! Oh my God! Treasure is about to rob my fuckin store! This is soooo damn cool!"

Treasure frowned at the white girl behind the counter and shook her head slowly. "Fine, fill up the biggest damn bag you got then since you giving it away!"

The white girl behind the counter emptied the contents of the register into a bag and then she paused. She looked around the store to make sure nobody was looking, then she looked at Treasure. "You know… we have a lot more money in the back office. Fuck it, take it all Treasure! You're my fuckin shero!"

———————

Treasure pulled out of the gas station parking lot with a bag full of money that she believed was close to $100,000. She was shocked that the gas station clerk had given up her father's entire stash for the day, and thought that she was trying to set her up. And no way was she going for that.

"Pweeese! Pweeese!" The gas station clerk screamed from her backseat. "Pweese yet me gwooo! Pweese!"

Treasure had duct-taped the gas station clerk and thrown her in the back seat of her own car. She had no sympathy and no remorse. She didn't feel as though she could trust anyone, and since she didn't feel as though she could trust anyone; she knew that every person must be accounted for. She felt like the girl could be giving up $100,000 of her father's gas station money in order to gain the million-dollar reward that the government had out for her. *Fuck that!*

Treasure stopped at the red light right beside the store and almost had a heart attack when she saw the police cars coming out of nowhere with their lights flashing. They were coming from all directions, and she thought for sure she had been caught, but the cops were simply headed to the store she had just left from. She watched as the cops drew their weapons and ran into the store, some of them going to the back entrance. She shook her head. *I knew this bitch was trying to set me up!*

Treasure ran the light and hit the expressway. She was going to have to try something bold in order to survive. She was going to have to get a hotel room right by the police station. They would never think to search for her over there. As far her hostage… She was going to make her suffer for trying her.

———————

Nerow was on the freeway on his way to Milwaukee, Wisconsin when the blue lights got behind him. Angry and frustrated, he pulled over. He knew he wasn't supposed to be headed out of Madison, so he tried to think of an excuse that would satisfy the cops.

"Hey sir. You are aware that your vehicle is being tracked by the vice department and that you are supposed to be on duty in the city of Madison, Wisconsin right?"

Nerow nearly chocked trying to get his lie out. "Yessir but I-"

"No sir. You've violated the vice contract and we're going to have to bring you in sir. Once you violate this contract, there is nothing that can save you. Step out of the car."

"Wait officer. I have a-"

"No sir. You have the right to remain silent. Anything you say-"

"I have her officer! I have her! I got her to trust me, and I didn't know where else to hide out at, so I was going to Milwaukee. I'm able to get her tonight actually. Or I can even bring her in tomorrow. Plus I know some other stuff going on in Madison. A few meth labs. Some coke spots. A few places that can get you a promotion!"

The officer paused when he heard the word promotion, as it was music to his ears. "A few meth labs huh? Make sure you write this statement down and give me the credit for it. I'm going to turn this in to my sergeant."

The officer stared at the statement that Nerow had written, and re-read it until he was satisfied. "OK sign your name right here, put the time and the date on it."

Nerow did as he was told and watched as a smile formed on the officer's face. The officer's greed was evident and pathetic. "Alright sir. You have a nice night and be safe!" He said as he made his way back to the patrol car.

Nerow knew that the white Challenger was supposed to be ditched a long time ago, but he knew that as soon as he did it; he was going to have a whole new set of problems on his hands. He sat there in the car and weighed his options.

Damn. Do I turn Salisha in and go on about my life, or do I keep Salisha in my life and say fuck my wack ass wife? Damn I miss my family right now though. What the fuck do I do?

A white OJ Simpson styled Bronco with loud mufflers pulled up to the store where Salisha was standing. The passenger side door opened and a petite white girl jumped out with long brunette hair. The driver's side door opened and another petite white girl with blond hair jumped out. They walked up to Salisha and stared at her.

Salisha stared back at them. "What the fuck do y'all motherfuckers want?"

The girl with brunette hair extended her hand for Salisha to shake it. "My name is Joshua."

Salisha frowned at the girl like she was crazy. She looked at the girl's hand like it was the scum of the earth. "You're a grown woman calling yourself Joshua? Or are you a man?"

The girl ignored Salisha and moved aside so the other girl could approach her. The girl with the blond hair looked into Salisha's eyes with eyes just as intense. "Bitch my name is Jack, and yes we're women. But you better get with the motherfucking program if you plan on staying free out here in these here streets! We're the Crazy White Boys."

Salisha's mouth opened wide and her cell phone slipped out of her hand and cracked against the cement. Her eyes were just as wide, rivaling her mouth. "Well I'll be damned! The Crazy White Boys huh? I have officially seen it all!"

By the time Treasure made it to the hotel near the police station, her idea had flown completely out of the window. Just the memory of her face being shown on those high definition televisions told her that she couldn't walk into any business establishment in the world without being noticed. She drove by the hotel slowly, looking to see what kind of activity was going on over there; and almost ran into a white Dodge Challenger by accident. The Challenger was turning into the police station and Treasure didn't even know its signal light was on. She hit the brakes and waited on the car to turn. Then she went down the street and turned around. When she got by the police station again, the guy had gotten out of the Challenger and was flipping her a bird.

"Fuck you too motherfucker!" Treasure said as she continued to drive the stolen car. She needed to come up with a plan, but she wasn't prepared to form a great plan since she hadn't been following the news like she normally did. Quickly, she turned the radio on and scrolled to a local news radio show.

"The crime rate has increased tremendously in the past thirty six hours, and we must do something about that immediately. Madison is not known for dangerous crimes, and we are going to do everything in our power to keep our city that way. This is Sergeant Mometta and I promise you that I'm going to find the culprits terrorizing the city. I promise you."

Treasure rolled her eyes as she listened to sergeant boast and lie about what he was going to do. She wanted to get the hell out of the city, but she knew that if she was to expect someone to be loyal to her; then she must exhibit loyalty to them. She absolutely *had* to tell Salisha about the snitching going on. If she didn't tell her, she could end up going back to prison; and she wasn't going to allow that.

"Pweeese yet me gwooooo! Pweeese!" The store clerk kept screaming.

Treasure drove until she saw a vacant back alley. She turned the car down the alley and put it in park. "Pweeese! Pweeese!" The clerk kept screaming.

Treasure turned and faced her with a straight face. "Didn't I tell you to shut the fuck up? I'm trying to think bitch!"

She placed her hand on the duct tape on the girl's mouth and before she pulled it, she gave her a warning. "If you scream, my gun will scream with you. Let this be my only warning." Treasure ripped the duct tape off of the girl's mouth and she let out the most blood curdling screams she could possibly make.

"Aaaaarghhhh!"

Wham! Wham! Wham! Wham! Wham! "Bitch, the fuck you thought was going to happen? You dumb ass! Ugh!" Treasure was angry that she'd had to waste her bullets and her time fucking with someone who didn't want to listen. All she had to do was pay attention and she would have let her ass go.

Treasure opened the door and kicked the girl's dead body onto the ground. She shut the door back and drove off into the night. She could focus a bit clearer now without all of the screaming in her ear.

———————

The Crazy White Boys had a trailer on the outskirts of the city where they rested. They let Salisha come in and make herself comfortable on their sofa for the rest of the night. As far as they were concerned, they didn't give a fuck if Salisha left out of the trailer and never came back. All they were trying to do was do as Mazzy asked them to do, and the rest was up to Salisha.

The next morning, the Crazy White Boys were up at 8 A.M. They woke Salisha up and told her plain and simple. "It's time to go to work."

"Work?" Salisha asked as she wiped the cold out of her eyes. "What the hell kind of work y'all got for me?"

———————

They arrived at Wells Fargo about an hour and a half after waking Salisha up out of her sleep. She sat in the Bronco looking as if she was in the middle of a bad nightmare. "Y'all bout to hit the fucking Wells Fargo? And then it's outside of a shopping mall? What the fuck? Man... I don't know about this shit yo. This shit is wild crazy! We don't even have a fuckin plan!"

Joshua and Jack got out of the Bronco and stared at Salisha until she got out of the SUV. Joshua reached into a box and pulled out three vests. She put one of them on, handed one to Jack, and handed the other one to Salisha.

Jack took a long irritated sigh and stared at Salisha. "Listen! We been doing this shit for years and we already have a fucking plan. The plan is to get your ass in and get your ass out, easy and simple. And if shit don't go right with us getting our money, then shit don't go right in nobody's lives today!"

Salisha didn't know what the hell they were talking about, so she put the vest on just following their leads. "OK pass me a strap and let's get it!"

Joshua stared at her like she was crazy. "The fuck you mean pass you a strap? That vest don't strap up or something?"

Salisha rolled her eyes. "Man please. That's not what I'm talking about. Yea the vest fits, but I'm talking about a pistol so we can get this shit cracking!"

Jack and Joshua burst out laughing listening to Salisha ask about a gun.

Joshua grabbed her plastic remote and led the way to the bank. "We already strapped Salisha!" She said forcefully.

Salisha stopped and watched them walk away from her and head to the bank. "What the fuck you mean *we strapped*? I ain't got shit on me! We ain't even got no ski-masks. You wanna just rob this shit bare-faced? NIggaz don't even go in pussy no more without protections!"

Joshua turned around and walked up to Salisha. She opened her vest up showing off her full attachment of explosives. "Bitch we all got bombs in this bitch! We about this money for real! It's either get rich or die for us! Bring your ass on bitch! If I hit

David Weaver

the switch on this remote, everybody will blow the fuck up so I suggest you get with the program like right now!"

Salisha had never been more afraid in all of her days. *I'm too old for this shit! Oh my God! Explosives?* Not wanting to piss off the Crazy White Boys any further, she followed the girls into the bank nervous as hell.

Joshua and Jack approached the bank manager silently and unassuming. Salisha wasn't far behind them. She didn't know if she was supposed to be right there with them, or if she was supposed to fall back.

"Hi, how may I help you lovely ladies today?"

Jack smiled at the poor woman. "O.K. You see this?" She asked, opening her vest up. "We are prepared to die like the Taliban right now. You are going to walk up to each person behind the counter and tell them not to hit the panic button. You are going to be responsible for the lives of everyone on the premises. If you fuck up, then everybody dies; us included. I will blow this bitch to smithereens with the tap of this button."

The ladies face turned tomato red as she stood there staring at the beautiful women. She couldn't believe what she was hearing. "Yes ma'am. I understand."

Before she walked off, Joshua stopped her. "Listen bitch. While you're at it, you rob the bank for us. Fill these bags with money and no dye packs. Fill these bags with money and do not put any fake money or tracking devices in the bag. Because I'm telling you right now, I am going to come back and blow this bitch up I swear to God. If there are officers outside waiting on me when I get out, I'm running back in and we'll all go to hell together!"

Sweat had collected on the lady's forehead and was rolling down the side of her neck as she listened to her instructions. "Yes. It's understood!"

Jack and Joshua stood there patiently while waiting on the manager to rob the bank for them. A lady was trying to get by the three women, and they didn't know it. "Excuse me, can you all move back out the way? Thank you."

Jack turned and looked in the face of the bank's assistant manager. She couldn't believe how arrogant she was. Jack opened her vest wide for the assistant

David Weaver

manager to see. Red, black, and royal blue wires were attached to square black packets; and everything was carefully attached to the lining of the inside of the vest. Each black packet had a red blinking light on it and there was a small blue light that didn't blink.

The assistant manager stared at her with a confused look on her face. Jack snapped. "I'll blow this bitch up right now! Right now! She ran into the lady, knocking her on the ground maliciously. She stood over her screaming. "I'll kill me bitch! I'll kill everybody in here!"

Joshua took a note out of Jack's playbook and did the same thing. She opened her vest up and ran around the bank with the remote in her hand. "I'll kill everybody! Right now! We don't wanna live! Fuck everything!"

Salisha felt a warm stream of urine trickle down her thighs and form a puddle on the floor where she was standing. The shit those girls were doing had scared her out of her mind. She had done plenty of wild shit in her life, but she had never robbed a bank; and had certainly never done so by threatening to blow her damn self up. *God please help me make it out of here alive. Please.*

The manager brought the bag of money back to Salisha, and it finally struck her that their work was done already. "Hey let's go!"

All three of the ladies started running towards the Bronco, and when they got there; an officer was standing there writing something down on a pad.

"May I help you officer?" Joshua asked politely.

The officer frowned as he tore off a ticket. "Yea, you can help me by paying this fine. You parked in the handicapped spot." He arrogantly handed Joshua the ticket, and turned to walk away. The three ladies got into the vehicle without him even noticing the big trash bag that Salisha was carrying. Salisha climbed into the backseat and slammed the door.

Her adrenaline rush was beyond powerful as she stared inside that huge bag filled with cash. Jack calmly drove out of the parking lot and got on the road headed back to the trailer. Neither one of the ladies said a word. Neither of them even mentioned the robbery. They were relaxed as if it was *normal* that they had just robbed a bank with explosives

David Weaver

attached to them. They were relaxed like they had just shot a scene out of a movie instead of just lived moments out of their lives.

Joshua pulled her vest off and handed it to Salisha, and Jack did the same thing. Without looking back, Jack said "Place those vests in that green gym bag on the floor."

Salisha scanned the floor for the gym bag and spotted it. She started to reach for it, but almost fell on the floor when Jack turned the vehicle into the driveway of their trailer. They were back at their home in one piece. Salisha grabbed the bag and opened it, and the first thing she saw was a .45 Glock. She pulled her vest off so that she could put it in the bag also. Jack handed Salisha the controller to the bombs and opened the door so that she could get out.

Salisha discreetly and quickly tucked the .45 Glock into her waistband, and stuffed all of the vests and the controller inside of the bag.

Jack picked up the bag of money, and her and Joshua walked inside of the trailer. Salisha quickly pulled the gun out to see if it was loaded or not. It was. She wasn't with the explosives and the *I'ma kill myself and you too* style shit, she was old school and didn't want to offer her own life trying to get money.

She went inside the house and sat down across from the ladies as they silently counted the money up.

"It's like $150,000 right here in this bag." Joshua said.

Salisha's eyes grew huge. "That's $50K each! Damn! Let me get mine now!"

Jack shook her head. "No, you have to pay Mazzy on your first job. So she gets your $50,000 this go-round. You get paid on the next two jobs, but you'll have to pay her again on the 4th job, and that's how the pattern goes."

Salisha was insulted. "Man Mazzy don't know we robbed a bank and got away with $150,000. And I damn sure didn't risk my life with explosives and shit to give away $50,000 of my money!"

Joshua sat back against the sofa. "The police officer who wrote me the ticket was Mazzy's husband. He let us go freely. There's levels to this shit, and you need to learn how this shit works if you ever plan on being anything other than a bottom feeding street bitch."

Salisha put her face in her hands and started shaking. Oh my God! I've been in prison too fucking long! How am I letting these white bitches call me out of my name? Man this is some bullshit! Oh my God! Oh my God!

Without thinking further, Salisha pulled her pistol out and pointed it the Crazy White Boys. "Put the keys on the table hoes. I told you I ain't giving Mazzy shit! As a matter of fact, I'm gon' take the entire lick! All $150,000. Fuck y'all!"

Joshua shook her head. "I knew you was going to do this. This is the type of shit that weak bitches do anyways. Go ahead and take the money and get the fuck off of my property. Get the-"

Wham! Wham!

Two bullets from the gun opened her head like a Corn Flake box. Jack's calm demeanor vanished as she watched her sister shake and convulse as if she was having a reverse orgasm. Finally Joshua collapsed and fell to the floor, the sound of her lifeless corpse smacking against it sounded like 100 hands simultaneously combining for one clap.

Salisha trained the pistol on Jack, and she was ready to fire.

"Wait Salisha! Please wait! I can be a major benefit to you alive! Mazzy is going to be by here in the next 30 minutes to an hour, and if at least one of us isn't alive; she's going to turn you over to the authorities. She's not going to go for you killing us because we've been paying her and her husband for years now. I'm telling you that this is not the smart thing to do."

Salisha listened to her and thought about it. "Well strapping me up with a fucking bomb like the got damn Taliban wasn't a smart idea either, and you still did it!"

All evidence of being a gangster left out of Jack's voice and the pure white girl within her came flowing out. "Salisha I am so darned sorry! Gosh. Please spare me and allow me to assist you with future endeavors. I have lots of things that I am able to assist you with if you would please give me an opportunity."

David Weaver

Salisha laughed at the tone of voice she was using. "You're funny Jack." She said as she lowered her pistol. She relaxed and laughed some more. She glanced around the room and by the time she looked back at Jack, she had a pistol pointed at her.

"You went for that shit?" *Wham!* A bullet struck Salisha in the shoulder and caused her to flip over the sofa backwards. Still conscious, Salisha rolled over and started firing through the sofa in the direction of where she estimated Jack was sitting.

"Ouch!" She heard Jack scream out. That's when she knew she had her. She stood up with her pistol stretched out, and saw blood rushing out of Jack's chest. Jack was trying to lift her gun up, but the pain wasn't allowing her to raise it properly. Salisha emptied her pistol. *Wham! Wham! Wham! Click! Click!*

"Shit!" Salisha thought to herself as she stared at the two dead white girls laying on the sofa. She had to get that bag of money and get the fuck out of the city because she wanted none of those kinds of problems in her life. If she got caught she knew they wouldn't hesitate to give her the death penalty for her crimes.

One glance at her criminal history and they would forever consider her a threat to all of white America, even though she didn't feel as though she was racist to any extent. She grabbed the keys off the table and the bag of money and ran to the Bronco. She tossed the bag of money in the backseat and looked down at the bag containing the explosives. She grabbed the bag to see if there were any more guns in it, but there were none.

She threw the bag on the ground and turned to go back inside of the house. She rummaged through the rooms of the trailer until she found what she was looking for. Her eyes got as big as the moon when she saw it. It was a gold plated AK-47. At first she thought maybe it was just a collector's item and that it wasn't real, but when she checked and saw that it was fully loaded she almost had an orgasm.

She aimed at the wall, pulled the trigger and 6 rounds went off in a split second. The holes were so big that they let the sun shine through. She was in love.

She turned to leave out and stopped once she got into the living room. Outside she saw Mazzy getting out of her car and walking up to the house.

David Weaver

Damn!

_____

Treasure ended up ditching the clerk's stolen car and hot-wired a car from a used car dealership. She'd become an expert at removing the tracking devices from new cars, but she just hated the fact that it took up a lot of her time. However, that used car dealership didn't even have tracking devices installed on their cars.

She'd stolen a plain white Mercury Tracer from the lot and drove to the nearest truck driver rest stop. Instead of parking with the rest of the cars, she drove the car until she was positioned behind the 18-wheeler trailers. It was there that she was able to catch up on sleep for a few hours.

_____

A knock on her window woke her up.

"Hey gal! That snitch in the truck in front of me just went and called the damned police on yer' ass! Said you fit the description of the gal who has been on the run and he's out to collect his damn reward!"

Treasure jumped up and opened the door. "Excuse me?"

"I'm just trying to help yer' ass! You don't have to have an attitude with me!" The truck driver said as he walked back to his truck.

Treasure was confused. She looked around and saw a white man pointing towards her car and panicked. She grabbed her bag of money and her gun, then discreetly slid over and opened the passenger side door. In the clearing was nothing but trees as far as she could see, but she knew that the police dogs would track her down easily. They had more energy than she had. She stepped out of the car and crouched down.

There were two big trucks on her left and two big trucks on her right. The guy who'd knocked on her window had gotten into the 3rd truck and started the engine. She didn't have time to figure out if he was trying to set her up or not. She just needed desperately to trust somebody in the world, and she was hoping that it could be him, even if for a little while.

She ran and jumped on the step-ladder just as he was about to pull off. She tapped on the window just as he had earlier, and when he saw her he hurriedly reached over to open the door for her. She maneuvered her way into the cab of the truck and dropped the bag of money on the floor.

"Please, I don't care how much you charge and I don't care where you're going! Just get me the fuck away from here!" Treasure screamed, exhausted.

The truck driver placed his hat on and shunned her. "I'll help you. I won't charge you anything. I'm headed to Florida though. You alright with that?"

Florida? Damnit! "Alright I'm fine with Florida. Let's go! I'll go anywhere if I can get the fuck away from this damned place!"

As soon as Mazzy made it to the front door, Salisha started blasting. She didn't have time to talk or conversate, she just fired away. She shot through the door, not necessarily trying to shoot her; but trying to let her know that when she came outside it was going down.

She stepped out and saw Mazzy on her knees praying and sweating. "Bitch what you praying for?"

Mazzy looked up, happy to see that it was Salisha who was holding the gun instead of the Crazy White Boys. She always knew the day was going to come where they were going to try to cross her out. "Salisha! Them bitches just tried to kill me! Did you shoot em?"

Salisha laughed at Mazzy. "Yea I shot they motherfucking ass alright. And I tried to blow your motherfucking scalp off too!"

Mazzy was shocked. "What? Me? Salisha we go way back, so I have absolutely no idea why you would want me dead. I'm helping you out when nobody else will. I'm on your side Salisha!"

Salisha shook her head. "You're not on my side. You're on your own side, and you're only looking out for your damn self. You don't give a fuck about me."

"I'm telling you Salisha! If you kill me, then my husband will know it's you! He'll come over here and see that you've killed our two partners and see that you've killed me also. The biggest manhunt in history will be on your ass if you do it. You can't-"

Tock-Tock-Tock-Tock-Tock!

She didn't even consider thinking about the things that Mazzy was trying to feed her. To her ears, it was just a bunch of bullshit.

She ran to the Bronco and cranked it up. She drove further to the outskirts of Madison until she seen some signs that said *Private Property*. She didn't know whose private property it was, but she did know that she needed a place where she could relax for a second. She needed to think without being rushed, and the private property indicator seemed like it would be the perfect location.

She drove down the path through the trees and parked. She lay back in her seat and closed her eyes for a second. She cried as she thought about everything that she'd had to do once she left prison. She thought about how difficult her life had become, and how she had to take people's lives just to survive. She hated being responsible for death, and at her age; she knew it would do nothing but bring on more bad luck.

She cried and cried. She remembered seeing Mazzy pray just before she took her life and that made her feel even worse. She clasped her hands together and closed her eyes. She prayed for forgiveness and understanding. She knew that nobody would be able to understand her except God almighty because He made her. She didn't know who else in the world would take her more serious than Him and only Him. She needed help. She needed assistance.

She thought about Nerow.

She remembered the passionate way he'd kissed her when they last saw each other and a surge of hope went through her body. She grabbed her cell phone and sat there for a moment trying to remember how he'd told her to contact him. Her mind was completely blank. She took a deep breath and stared at the phone a little longer.

She rubbed her fingers across the keypad slowly until it came to her. She pressed and held down the speed dial number. Seven. She needed Nerow to come save her immediately.

David Weaver

Treasure lay back in the uncomfortable seat and stared at the passing scenery. She wondered if fighting so hard to remain free was worth it or if she should just turn herself in and get it over with. At that point she was mentally exhausted. She didn't have anyone special to turn to in her time of need, and it seemed like she was stealing another car every day.

She had to rob for cash, and kill innocent people in order to escape tight situations. She had ruined many families and it was beginning to cause some severe wear and tear on her soul. She was so tired, but every time she thought back to how she had to live like an animal in the prison cell; she knew that she couldn't go back. She knew that if she went back after all of the bad things she had done, that things were going to be unbearably worse.

The truck driver attempted to make small talk but it was obvious that Treasure wasn't interested in communicating too much. He turned the radio on and continued to focus on the road.

"Today in Madison, Wisconsin the infamous gang, the *Lipstick Clique* has struck again. Treasure is a prison escapee who has been managing to avoid the clutches of the justice system for quite some time now; and it has begun to become embarrassing for the Federal Bureau of Investigations. The director of the FBI had this statement to relay to the public:

"At this point we have had it up to here! Today the Lipstick Clique killed the innocent daughter of a Senator. Her name was Ashley and she worked in her father's convenience store on evenings when she didn't have to study for school. She was majoring in psychology when one of the members of the Lipstick Clique shot her dead! I have had a conversation with the President of the United States of America, and he has given me every resource that I could possibly ask for so that we can help capture this fugitive and her sidekick.

We are prepared to pay you your asking price! All I ask is that you look around you right now! Somebody out there has to see her! Just send a text message, email or give 1-800-Most-Wanted a call right now! Help us! We will pay you your asking price! If you can deliver her to us we are prepared to pay you millions. Help us please!"

"That was Senator Cosby relaying that message to the public. From the reports, the other member of the Lipstick Clique gang has been on a murderous spree also. She has murdered three women since her release from prison, including the wife of a local Madison detective. She assisted in an armed bank robbery at Wells Fargo earlier with explosives strapped to her vest, and killed the people who aided in the robbery hours later. She is ruthless."

The truck driver reached and turned the dial on the radio. The more he listened to them talk, the more nervous he became.

"So why don't you just turn me in and get rich?" Treasure asked as she stared at the man out of the side of her eye. "What the fuck do you think you're getting by helping me? Pussy? You want me to suck your dick? What do you want from me?"

The old man kept driving the truck, ignoring the questions that Treasure was asking him. She stared at him for a while, then pulled out her pistol and sat it on her thigh. The man glanced over at the pistol and kept driving as if he didn't see it to begin with.

"Why the fuck are you helping me?" Treasure asked again. "Do you have cops in the back of the truck? Fuck this! Tell them to get me now!" She screamed violently. "Fuck you and fuck everybody!"

The traffic was light on the expressway, and the man was fully focused. He listened to Treasure vent in a crazed rage, and as soon as she started to calm down he responded. "I've been on the run from the state prison for ten years now. I killed my wife for double-crossing me. I knew the only way to beat the double cross was with the triple cross. So I stabbed three crosses in her chest and watched her bleed to fuckin death."

The truck was studio booth silent as the truck continued to inch its way across America. For the first time in a long time, both of them were stunned and speechless. Treasure had questions, but she didn't want to ask because she had met someone on the same level as her. He wanted to ask her questions also, but he knew to observe the criminal's rulebook.

Nobody said a word until they crossed into Georgia. Treasure had noticed that the driver was swerving and became curious about his condition.

"Do you need to take a rest?" She asked, concerned.

He sat up instantly. He straightened the wheel out on the vehicle and continued to drive. He looked down and looked back up. "Yea we're going to have

David Weaver

to ditch this shit anyways. You're going to have to go your way and I'm going to have to go my way. I don't ever want to see you again and I don't ever want to be involved in the dumb ass shit you got going on. I killed somebody for a purpose and for a reason. You and your friends killed people for fun."

"What the fuck is you talking about?" Treasure snapped as her attitude made its sunrise over her body.

The man pulled into the first available rest stop and started unbuckling his seat belt. "Ok I tried to speak to you when we first left Madison but you didn't wanna talk. This ain't my truck. Shit I haven't had a truck since before I went to prison! I stole this shit from the rest stop, and since both of us were on the run I said fuck it!"

"What? You did what! Damnit! Now they're going to know where the fuck I am! You bastard! They're going to think I stole the fuckin truck!" Treasure screamed.

"Right!" The man hollered back. "If you're going to be a criminal, you must learn to think like a criminal at all times and not just sometimes! You're lucky I didn't get pulled over. Your crimes are far

David Weaver   106

greater than my crimes. They would have been happy to have you, and I probably would have been able to drive the hell off."

Treasure pointed her gun at him carefully. "Give me your gun."

"Huh? I don't have no gun!"

She pulled the trigger and fired a bullet into the door that he was leaning on. "All criminals have guns. Give me your fuckin' gun now!"

The truck driver started to reach into the center console to give her the pistol when she fired another shot into the door. He froze. "What the hell you want me to do now?" He asked.

"Just hold still motherfucker! I'll get the shit! You don't move!"

Treasure reached into the console and pulled out a chrome-plated 9 mm.

"But why the fuck are you taking my gun from me?" The truck driver asked.

"Because you were going to rob me for my money! That's not going to happen! I'm the robber!"

He exhaled. "You're taking this a little bit too far. I have my own bag of money! See?" He reached back into the center console and pulled out a black plastic bag and sat it in his lap. "I wasn't going to rob you!"

Treasure grinned at him. "But I'm definitely going to rob your ass!"

The man reached for the door handle, and the bullets turned him into a statue. Treasure shot him so easily that it was like she only tapped him on the shoulder. She was angry that he had traveled across America in a vehicle that *he* had stolen. She looked at the mile meter in the middle of the vehicle and panicked when she saw the distance and exact location of the vehicle on the computer display.

She knew that the company who owned the truck was just waiting on the truck to park so that the police could make their arrest. But as sleepy as she was, she would have to be completely dead in order to just lay there and allow that to happen. She threw his bag of money inside of her bigger bag. She jumped out of the truck and took off running.

"Fuck you bitch!" Nerow screamed as he pointed his index finger in his wife's face. "You were going to leave me without even hearing the fucking story! I should have known you wasn't shit! I married the wrong bitch!"

"Nerow I'm sorry!" I just didn't know what to do! I'm so sorry! Please forgive me!"

"I said fuck you!"

Nerow walked out of the house for what he knew was going to be the last time. He slammed the door and jumped into the white Challenger. He was going to get with the love of his life and live on the run forever. He was never going to trust anyone else in the world besides Salisha. *Fuck everyone!*

As soon as he started the car up, his phone rang.

"Hello?"

"This is Detective McHenry. Look. That woman we're looking for has killed my wife!" The detective's voice was hoarse as if he had been screaming for hours. "So if you can't get bring her to me, your ass is going the fuck down! I'm going to make everybody pay for this shit! You have two hours!" The detective hung up the phone without giving Nerow a chance to respond.

Nerow laughed at the phone call and shook his head. Motherfuck the police! They're going to have to catch me in Timbuktu. They lucky I don't go back in this house and off that backstabbing bitch!

He placed his foot on the brakes and prepared to shift the car into drive when the phone rang again.

"Hello?"

"Nerow!"

"Salisha?"

"I love you so much Nerow! Please come save me. Please take me with you. I just got out of prison and my world is falling apart. I don't have anyone I can trust except for you. I just wanna be in your arms."

Nerow smiled as he listened to his true ride or die chick confess her love for him. "I love you too baby. I'm going to go handle a couple of things and then hit you back-"

"No!" Salisha cried out desperately.

"What's wrong baby?"

Salisha hesitated for a second. She thought about the words that she was about to speak, and felt in her heart that he was the correct person; and the only person that she could ever speak them to.

"Shit Nerow. I done killed like three motherfuckers in the past hour! I gotta get the fuck out the city like right now!"

Nerow almost swallowed his tongue. The detective that called him was only concerned about his wife being dead, so he had no idea that Salisha was on a serial killer mission. He kept his composure and gathered his thoughts. No matter what she had done, she was still the love of his life. She was his one true ride or die chick and he wasn't about to give that up for anything in the world.

"O.K. where are you Salisha?"

"Shit I don't know! I'm in the got damn woods somewhere with a big bag full of money."

"Alright look. If you have a gun, just drop it wherever you are. Keep the money in your possession. I want you to walk further into the woods maybe like 30 to 40 feet. Then I want you to make a

111   David Weaver

seven feet path to the left and a seven feet path to the right. Just kick some dirt up so it'll confuse the police dogs. Then I want you to go back down the 40 feet path, walk right past the gun and go across the street. Go through the trees in the opposite direction and stay quiet until you hear my voice.

I'm going to track your phone with the GPS. I'll get you and we can get the fuck out the city. Don't worry about shit! You're in the hands of a real nigga! Ain't nobody going to fuck with you! I'ma keep you safe for the rest of your life!" Nerow boasted.

Salisha was nervous about leaving her weapon behind, but she felt like if she wasn't going to trust Nerow right then, then she wasn't going to be able to trust anybody ever again. And not being able to trust anyone was certainly not a good feeling. She *needed* to trust someone. *Immediately.*

She tossed the gun down and did as Nerow asked her to do. She followed love.

––––––––

Salisha stared down at her jailhouse jumpsuit in a trance. She couldn't believe she had fallen for

David Weaver   112

Nerow's bullshit! He had played his cards close to his chest, and only fed her the cards that she wanted to possess. But when it was time for her to display her hand, those weren't the cards that she needed in order to win the game. Tears rolled down her face in a steady and slow stream as she sat on her top bunk in the jailhouse.

Her cellmate walked into the room and grabbed her cup. "You still crying because that nigga tricked your ass? I already told you fuck that nigga. I know it hurts, but you can't cry over what you can't control."

She knew that already, but hearing somebody say it who hadn't been in her shoes held no effect. She thought about how perfect Nerow had played her.

He'd come through like a knight in shining armor when she was in the bushes hiding. Like a gentleman he carried her bag of money for her to his white car. He placed it in the trunk, gave her a hug and a kiss and went to the driver's side of the car. He opened the door and waited until she walked to the passenger side door.

She pulled the door handle and it was locked. "Nerow, unlock the door baby."

David Weaver

He'd sat there fumbling with buttons and acting like he was trying to unlock the door, but in reality was stalling for time. In no time, officers had surrounded her; and she was unarmed. The murder weapon was across the street and she was standing there red handed. She remembered staring at Nerow with confusion on her face, and remembered the smirk that he gave back to her.

Her facial expression read: How could you?

His facial expression answered: Easy!

She thought about how he didn't give a fuck about her and had left her for dead. He'd put her into position to receive the death penalty, and had robbed her of her money in the process. She hated the fact that he had betrayed her so deeply, but there was nothing she could do about it except cry. There was no way she was going to be able to get out of the deep shit Nerow had put her in.

But if there ever became a way, she knew she was going to kill him dead.

"Salisha!" One of the inmates called out. "Come get your legal mail!"

Salisha went out into the dayroom where the correctional officer was handling mail call. She walked up and showed her the jailhouse identification card that she had been given. She signed for her letter and went back to the cell. She climbed on top of the bed and opened it, knowing that it was going to be a plea deal for her to accept a life sentence instead of the death penalty.

WE ARE PREPARED TO OFFER YOU A MORE LENIENT SENTENCE AND POSSIBLY LET YOU OUT ON BAIL IF YOU ARE WILLING TO ASSIST IN THE AID AND CAPTURE OF TREASURE. WE ARE AWARE THAT YOU AND HER ARE VERY CLOSE, AND WE HAVE RECEIVED THE GO-AHEAD FROM THE HIGHEST LADDER OF THE FEDERAL GOVERNMENT TO ASK YOU FOR ASSISTANCE. CALL THIS NUMBER IF YOU ARE INTERESTED. WE LOOK FORWARD TO HEARING FROM YOU.

Salisha ripped the letter to shreds without looking at the phone number. She was not a snitch and would never be one. She would forever be against the law and was going to stand up and take her punishment like a woman. She didn't give a fuck if it was the death penalty or a life sentence. At least she'd been able to go into McDonald's and place an order. That was a memory that was going to last her a lifetime. *Fuck the world.*

SECTION

TWO

Catfish punched the wooden wall like it was a punching bag. "Arrrrghhh!" He slammed his fist into it repeatedly as if it was only a pillow. Blood leaked out of his fists as he unleashed all of his pent-up aggression and frustration.

"Fuck!" He screamed as he alternated fists and continued punching until a chunk of the wall fell out. When the chunk fell out, he switched to another section and repeated the same exact process. His fists were swollen and his voice was hoarse from all of the hollering he had been doing.

David Weaver

At last he was exhausted. He sat down on his bed and placed his face into his palms. He had never completely gotten over the fact that his wife was gone, and being that he was a family man it was foreign to him to not have a lady on his side. He'd attempted to date someone since he'd been in the Philippines, but the lady just didn't have enough backbone.

He thought about his wife and all of the beautiful memories that she'd brought into his life. She was such a special lady to him. She was the lady that kept him balanced, and without that balance; he was deteriorating rapidly. He was losing weight in his face, and was barely coming out of his home. He was happy that Kyla and Malcolm were together and living happily ever after, but he was sad that he wasn't able to have a similar outcome with the love of his life.

He hadn't eaten in the past 24 hours, and knew that nothing was going to change anytime soon. He pulled his shoes off and got in his bed. He closed his eyes and searched for sleep. He found it for about ten seconds, but it ran from him. He concentrated harder, closed his eyes and chased behind the ever-elusive sleeping condition. He ran behind it until he caught it.

He grabbed it with two hands and held it in place. Finally he slept.

Treasure managed to take a taxicab into the city of Atlanta, GA. The excitement of the city seemed to energize her. There were so many young, black, and beautiful women there that she didn't feel like anyone would be able to pinpoint her as the lady on America's Most Wanted. For a minute she felt young again. For a minute she felt as though she had no responsibility whatsoever. She felt rich and carefree. She even felt like going out to have some fun that night.

She called another cab once she was in the city so that she could go visit the place she most wanted to visit before she died. *CNN.* She had been so infatuated with news programs that she just had to see the building in person. She was amazed at how quickly a news station could take a regular person and turn them into anything in the world that they chose them to be. That was the ultimate power.

Once the news said it, they didn't give a fuck what you said in response or who you gave her reply to. Their opinions were what mattered over everyone else's. Once they said it, even if it was false; it was true according to the public.

She sat down at a table at the CNN center and placed her bag of money between her legs. She opened her sandwich and prepared to eat lunch when déjà vu happened all over again. Her face was plastered across at least 40 television screens, but this time; they had up to the minute details.

"She was last seen stepping out of cab outside of the CNN center. Please call—"

Treasure grabbed her bag and knocked her chair and table over getting the fuck up out of there. She ran down the street and crossed through ongoing traffic as if she had the right to do so. She kept crossing sidewalks and main streets until she saw a group of homeless people sitting down in a circle listening to a portable radio.

She ran up to them without speaking and sat in the middle of them. The men and women were about to say something, but when she reached into her bag and pulled out several $20 bills everybody got quiet.

She listened to the old TLC song, "Waterfalls," until it went off. She didn't know the meaning of it, but she did know that the damn song sounded good as hell, until it was rudely interrupted.

"Breaking News! There is a dragnet over the city for a young female fugitive of justice. This lady is wanted all over the country for a strong stream of murders and robberies. She should be treated as armed and dangerous, and if you should be so unfortunate to see her; you need to alert authorities at your earliest convenience. Again, she has been spotted in the city of Atlanta GA. Do not attempt to stop her, simply alert authorities and they will handle the rest."

Awkwardly, Treasure casually glanced around the group of homeless men and women while they openly stared at her. Her heart was beating like a marching band as she sat there hoping they wouldn't put two and two together. She looked down the street to her right and saw officers walking and pointing. She looked across the street and saw officers looking in every direction possible. She looked to her left and saw officers walking up the street from that direction also.

The homeless lady she was sitting by tapped her on the shoulder. "You can get in my grocery cart and I'll cover you with a blanket. If you pay us good, we'll walk you straight out of this shit you're in."

Treasure glanced at her and knew that she didn't have any option but to trust her. She slid backwards until she was sitting on the ground. She clutched her bags in one arm and folded her petite body into the grocery cart that was sitting behind the group. Filthy blankets covered her world and as she lay there, half expecting the lady to turn her in, and half expecting to have to fire her pistol through the shopping cart holes.

The cart started rolling slowly, and Treasure could hear the footsteps of the homeless men and women walking on either side of the cart. She also heard the jangle of handcuff keys and approaching footsteps.

"That lady who was just sitting with you all. Where did she go?" One officer asked.

Treasure could feel the panic in the homeless lady's arm as she stood there shaking. She was terrified. "She... she took off running! She said she was about to steal a car. She went that way!"

Treasure held her breath for a second. Then she let go of her breath and held her pistol. *Fuck this shit, I'm firing!*

But as soon as she was getting ready to start firing her pistol, the keys and the heavy footsteps of the police took off running. *Wow!* Treasure thought as she felt her heart skip several beats. She lay there and listened to the sound of the road as the shopping cart pushed her deeper and deeper toward her freedom. After about ten minutes, the lady leaned close to the cart and whispered. "Baby girl, we're close to the Greyhound station. You're going to have to get out of the cart now. The coast is clear. And plus you're not the only criminal in the Greyhound vicinity, so you can relax a little."

Treasure tossed the smelly blanket aside and jumped out of the cart. She went inside of her bag and pulled out the bag of money that she'd robbed from the truck driver. She grabbed stacks of money and passed it around the circles as if it was a common cold. "Look, I don't know how much money that is; but I do know it is a lot. And I don't have no idea where the money came from because I robbed a robber for it."

David Weaver

The homeless men and women's eyes swelled in amazement. They only expected for her to give them $20 a piece, and here they were getting enough $20 bills to go buy a half a kilogram of cocaine. "Lady!" The oldest man spoke up. "If you need for us to do anything else, anything else in the world; what is it? We're going to help you out! You did more for us than the government has ever did, you feel me? Me and my potna' right here were in the war back in the days. And when it was time for us to get our checks from the military, Uncle Sam told us that they had no record of us ever being over there. Now ain't that some bullshit?"

Treasure stared into the man's eyes and saw that he was sincere. She stared at his friend's eyes and saw the same hurt and betrayal that she saw when she looked herself in the mirror. She knew they were for real. "Who are these ladies you have here with you?" She asked as she continued to stare in their eyes.

"This right here is my wife who pushed the cart and helped you get here." The man spoke again. Me and her have been through it all, and even though she could have gotten a better man, she still decided to stick by my side through thick and thin. She's a real rider. And if you ever find a love on that level, I want you to give it your all baby girl. I'm telling you now that these types of loves are extremely rare."

Treasure admired the long time lovers. She wanted the same thing out of life, and it was starting to get to the point where she thought she was going to have to go back to prison to find someone. *Men are going to forever double cross me as long as I'm worth millions of dollars to the government.* She smiled at the man and shook her head. "I salute you two. That's real love and I admire that."

The homeless lady blushed and smiled at her. "Why thank you. Love is never going to be easy, but the most difficult phases of your relationship will always create your truest memories. Find your love and live your life. Fuck what the police say. Are you sure you don't need anything else?"

Treasure stood there and studied the crowd around them. Nobody seemed to be paying them any attention at all. For a second she calmed down and analyzed her position. She looked at the bus and knew that she couldn't hop on it at that moment because there were pictures of her behind the counter. "Alright listen. I need for you to go get me three bus tickets. One for Philadelphia, one for Columbus, GA and one ticket for Jacksonville, Florida. I'll pay you when you bring the tickets." She said to the lady. The lady walked off promptly.

She looked at the homeless men. "Alright, I need y'all to go buy me a cell phone. Can I—"

"That's easy. My homeboy round the corner got them hot ass phones. You just buy the iPhone and it's on. No contract, no minutes; nothing! Those shits just work! He wants $1500 for them though."

Treasure exhaled. "Fine, get the phone and you shall have your money."

———

Salisha sat down at the activity table in the dayroom. Her cellmate ran out of her cell laughing. "Hey y'all! Y'all know that damn girl named Treasure?" The entire crowd of card players looked up from dealing and shuffling and focused on the inmate speaking.

"They on the news talking about they spotted her ass *outside* the CNN building in Atlanta GA. They say the officers had an accurate trail on her ass the

entire time, and then she disappeared into *thin air!*
Now y'all know that's a bad bitch!"

Salisha's spades partner laughed. "Damn right
she is. Who else breaks out of prison and lives a
public life? She's like a fucking celebrity bank
robber. What happened to the Lipstick Clique shit she
was running at one point? I don't hear much about
that any more. You heard anything?"

Salisha's cellmate shook her head. "Nah, and
honestly I don't give a fuck right now. This is the
Treasure show!"

Salisha picked up her cards and grinned. She was
rooting for Treasure to continue to outsmart those
motherfuckers. She was going to go to the grave
knowing that there was at least one person in the
world that she could trust. For a long time she
thought it was Treasure who was against her when
she was in the streets. But when she found out that it
was Nerow's bitch ass, she had to charge it to the
game.

It was her decision to trust that bitch made nigga.
And it was her decision and her decisions only that
had her back in her current predicament. *At least I got*

me some McDonald's though! Yea motherfuckers!
Ha!

Treasure let about four days lapse after her last sighting before she decided to finally board the Greyhound bus. She had elected to go to Columbus, GA since she had some unfinished business to tend to down there with her former lover. He'd signed his own death certificate when he tried to betray her love for his own benefit. She was going to make sure he felt the wrath of her pain.

While on the bus she started thinking about a long-term survival strategy. She didn't have a clique of criminals as she once had in the past, so she would have to look out for herself during every robbery she had to commit. She grew weary just thinking about it, and lay back in the seat in exhaustion.

She thought about the homeless men and women she ended up kicking it with over the past four days, and smiled at how trustworthy they were. For the first time in her life she had been able to sleep peacefully and not worry about anyone robbing her or turning her in to the authorities. She had helped them generously, and for that; they were never going to betray her or let anyone else betray her. She was like Ms. Robin Hood to them, a true princess amongst thieves.

Treasure glanced at the phone and thought deep. She remembered calling a phone number a long time ago in order to call upon a favor. Here she was again, in even deeper shit than she was when she first dialed the number. She needed assistance severely, but she knew that she had more than likely ruined her chances of getting help. The last time they asked her for help, she didn't feel that she was in a good enough position to comply. Turning them down and then asking them for help again... That didn't even sound right. She took a deep breath and dialed.

Kyla cradled her baby girl like the gift from God that she was. "Hey boo-boo! I love you boo-boo!" She said as she rubbed baby Majalla's hair. "I love you boo-boo!"

Her phone rang suddenly, startling her for a second because nobody ever called their house phone. She sat her daughter down and went to pick up the phone.

"Hello?"

"Hey. Ky?"

She listened to the American on the other end of the phone as he broke down the entire situation. At the end of him explaining what had taken place, he asked Kyla to write down a phone number.

"Who's number?"

"It's the girl's number I was telling you about who needed the help." The man said quickly.

"Treasure... yea... ok. Call it out again."

She wrote the number down and hung the phone up, rolling her eyes in the process. That bitch wouldn't help me, I don't know why she want our help again. The fuck she think this is?

Malcolm came in the house with a light layer of sweat glistening off his forehead. He went to the refrigerator, opened it and sat down without getting anything out.

"Is everything fine Mal?" Kyla asked her husband. "How did the doctor's visit go?"

"Everything is fine Kyla. Everything except for my ca..." He was about to tell her, but he couldn't bring himself to get it out.

"Except for what Malcolm? I didn't hear." Kyla said as she walked closer to the man of her dreams. "What did you say baby?"

"I said... Everything is fine except for my homey Catfish!" He said forcefully. It wasn't the truth, but it wasn't a lie either. He was shaken up about what the doctor had told him, but instead of worrying his wife about it, he thrust his frustration into the concerns of his best friend.

Kyla sat in Malcolm's lap and kissed him gently. "What's wrong baby? What's the matter with Catfish?"

Malcolm's world brightened when his wife showed him affection. There was nothing in the

David Weaver

entire universe that could make him happier than Kyla Powers. Not money, and not his namesake; power. Every day that he opened his eyes, he thanked God for putting him into such a blessed position.

"You know Catfish lost his wife baby. And he hasn't stopped beating himself up over that. He's hurt. I mean he's really hurt Kyla. I thought for a minute that he had gotten over it and moved on with his life, but it seems to be affecting him severely right now. For as long as I've known Catfish, I've never seen him in the state of mind that he is in now. He's not eating, not doing anything except for punishing himself.

And it's crazy because as powerful as I may be, even I myself am powerless to the muscle and the strongholds of love. We can have all the AK-47s in the world, but that little cartoon muthafucka' with the bow and arrow would kill us all. Cupid."

Kyla kissed Malcolm on the lips gently. "Baby… I know that's your best boy but you can't beat yourself up because of what happened."

Malcolm sighed and stared into her beautiful eyes. He intertwined his hand into hers and pulled her back against his broad chest. He kissed her on the temple and wrapped his arms around her.

She lay there peacefully, enjoying the results that her hard work and dedication had yielded. Yet she felt sorry for Catfish. She felt worse about the situation now that she was seeing the effects that his situation was having on her husband. She had to do something about it. Immediately.

––––––––––

Kyla came out of the house for her evening jog, and admired the beautiful Philippine sky before she took off. While jogging, she formulated a plan so that she could help out three people at the same exact time. *This could work!* She thought as she jogged to Catfish's residence. She didn't even have to worry about knocking, since he was sitting on the porch with his muscle shirt on.

As soon as he heard her footsteps he stood up. "Is everything ok Mrs. Powers?"

He was still Malcolm's best friend, and ever since him and Kyla got married; he had also become Kyla's best friend as well.

David Weaver

"No I'm afraid not Catfish. I—"

"Let me go get my shotgun!"

"Wait! Catfish listen!"

He turned around and stood in front of her, listening to what she had to say.

"There's this girl-"

"No Kyla! I'm not doing any more of your blind dates. None of them work because you don't know the tastes of my heart. Anyone can suggest a recipe, but just because the recipe sounds good to you doesn't mean that I'm not allergic to all of the ingredients."

Kyla stood there stunned. "Wow. I'm not trying to hook you up with anyone. I was presented with a dangerous mission and I was wondering if you knew of anyone who might be interested in taking it on."

"What kind of dangerous mission?" He asked, excitement entering his voice again. His eyes lit up like he'd just won the lottery for a hundred million dollars.

"It involves an old friend of the Bankroll Squad, and she's in America. I was wondering if you knew of anyone over there who could help her. You probably have heard the name if you still follow the American news."

"Of course I follow the news from my country." He said slowly. Just saying those words seemed to deflate him. His country was where his wife was. Dead. "Yea... I follow the damn news. Who is she?"

"Treasure."

Catfish stood there for a minute, then he started laughing. "Oh, you talking about that wild ass bandit girl. Lipstick Clique Treasure? I read up on her every day. That's like my entertainment. They can't catch her muthafuckin' ass for shit! She's bad! I think she's in Atlanta GA right now laying low. Watch! When she shows her head again, they'll think she's in Clinton, South Carolina and her ass will be in Clinton, Iowa! She's no joke!"

Kyla smiled as she listened to Catfish go on and on about Treasure. It was clear that he was already quite fond of her, but she didn't know how fond of her he was. She had a plan, but if it was going to work or not would be completely up to him.

David Weaver

"Yep, that's her. Treasure. And she's not in Atlanta GA, she's in Columbus, GA. She's looking for Malcolm's snitch ass brother so she can get revenge. She called on the squad for help because she feels like she's just running around like a chicken with its head cut off. She doesn't have a plan, and is just robbing everything in sight. I think she needs to be brought back here with us. She's loyal, and for that reason alone I want her to be a member of the world's most loyal organization. The Bankroll Squad."

Catfish stood there letting the words resonate. *Treasure. The Bankroll Squad.* "Damn that's a hot combination though. We should have had her on the squad instead of that Pam bitch!" Catfish vented. "If it wasn't for her ass, my wife would still be alive! I believe this in all of my heart! Fuckin' rat bitch!"

Kyla remained quiet as the same emotions that were flowing through Catfish overtook her body. She felt anger building up and had to let it go so that it wouldn't ruin her night.

"Yea, I know somebody over there who might be able to help her get back over here. I most certainly do." Catfish said.

"Alright, who is it?" Kyla asked.

"Me."

That was not how Kyla was intending for the conversation to go. She was hoping that Catfish really knew someone who could bring her back, that way Treasure and Catfish could fall in love right here on the Philippine island. "Hell nawl Catfish! Your ass can't go back to America! How the fuck you gon' go to a place we fought so hard to escape? That's the silliest shit in the world! I'm going to tell Malcolm!"

Catfish laughed gently. "You can go tell him, but by the time you leave and come back I'll be gone already. I need this in my life Kyla, you just don't understand how bad I needed something like this. This is going to help me get better. I look forward to meeting Treasure with her bad ass."

Kyla was against it. "You can't break into a country that wants you dead Catfish. They're going to kill you the first time they lay eyes on you. And it's not like you're a small guy. You're going to stand out in a crowd and it's going to be hard for you to get away. I really don't recommend this at all Catfish. Please don't go."

The Lipstick Clique II

Catfish simply stared at her. She knew that everything she was saying to him was going in one ear and flying out the other ear. He was completely intrigued by Treasure, and had a lusting thirst for the dehydration of danger. It was the perfect job for him.

"I already have a plan Kyla. Don't you go back and tell Malcolm nothing you hear me? Let me handle this."

Kyla shook her head. "I'm not going to stand here and lie to you Catfish. My husband is going to be the first and only person I tell. I hold no secrets from him."

Catfish smiled. "That's very respectable. I love y'all's relationship. It inspires me and lets me know that real love is possible if you have faith and believe. And I think… I believe… Let me go meet Treasure." He said as he turned to go back in his house.

Kyla was panicking. She knew that it was possibly the last time she would ever see Catfish again. America wanted him dead and they were not going to let him go if they caught him. She tried to speak but her voice got stuck in her throat. She was mad at herself for even bringing the situation to Catfish. That wasn't how she wanted it to go. *I can*

David Weaver   138

be such an airhead sometimes! I should have known he was going to do this!

"I'm going to fly in to Mexico and pay a friend of mine to smuggle me into Texas. From there I'll take the bus to Columbus, GA. I got this all under control Kyla. Relax, you know I do danger for a living."

Kyla scratched her head while trying to figure out how he effortlessly made the most dangerous plan in the world seem like a walk in the park. She started to protest, but didn't know what to say. She knew that she needed to get home as soon as possible to tell her husband what she'd done. *I hope he forgives me. Damn!*

"Kyla, are you going to give me her contact information or are you just going to stand there?"

She broke out of her daze and wrote the information down on a piece of paper. She stared at Catfish as he walked away and into his house. She put a cup on the piece of paper so it wouldn't blow away, and suddenly wished that she were as fragile as the paper itself. She wished she could blow away for what she thought she had done in error. She didn't mean to do it and hoped her husband would understand.

139   David Weaver

As fast as possible, she took off running back in the direction of their house.

About ten miles outside of Columbus GA, a set of police lights started flashing behind the Greyhound bus. Treasure saw them and knew immediately what it was about. She was already sitting in the last seat of the bus, so she pulled her pistol out, grabbed her bags and ducked down onto the floor. She thought about going in the bathroom stall, but knew that the officers were going to look in there.

She crawled under the seat in front of her until she hit someone's foot by accident. The man looked under the seat with a confused look on his face. "What are you do—"

But he didn't get a chance to say anything further, Treasure had a pistol pointed in his face. She held her finger up to her lips. "If you say anything, and if I get caught; I'm putting a bullet in the ass of everyone on the bus."

The officer stopped the bus and climbed aboard. He had a picture in his hand, and was walking down the aisles comparing everyone's faces to the picture that he was holding. By the time he got to the last seat he was pissed. "Damn!" He said and turned to leave off of the bus.

Treasure made a mistake. Her foot was hanging out from under the seat and she didn't know it. The officer tripped up and almost fell to the floor. Treasure hurriedly pulled her feet back under the seat and prayed that she didn't have to shoot up the bus. The officer caught his balance and turned around to address the situation at hand.

"Something wrong with your foot son?" The officer asked.

"No sir, nothing's wrong. I made a mistake when I was stretching. I didn't mean to trip you!"

"What the fuck is you sweating for son?"

The guy in the seat took a deep breath. "It's hot as hell back here and he don't have the air conditioning on. I sweat a lot as it is, and he got me sweating even more!"

The officer nodded his head. "Well alright son. I'll tell the bus driver to turn the air up a little bit. You have a good day!"

David Weaver

The man in the seat exhaled deeply once the bus took off again. Treasure got up off of the floor and sat in her seat. The man in the seat turned around and glared at her. "You almost got me busted bitch! I'm carrying two bricks of heroin on me! What the fuck was you thinking?" He snapped.

Treasure remained silent until they made it to the Columbus Greyhound station. She got off the bus and followed the guy with the two blocks of heroin into the men's bathroom stall. She pulled her pistol out easily. "Hand the work over then."

"Hell no! This shit is $160,000 worth of raw. You won't be getting this without at least giving me a bullet."

Wham!

Treasure let off a shot that split open the skin of his thigh like a piece of chicken. She reached out and relieved him of the backpack, adding to the bag she was already carrying. She already knew he was going to make her shoot him for the heroin. She knew based on her last visit to Columbus GA that it often took an actual bullet to get her point across appropriately. A lot of them niggas were straight up hardheaded.

She walked out of the men's bathroom as calm as she could be. There was no security in the run down station, so she knew that she would have no complications whatsoever. She walked outside of the station and got into an awaiting taxi.

"How are you young lady?" The cab driver asked.

She sighed. "I'm fine. Can you take me to Macon road please?"

He put the car in gear. "No problem at all. I've been here for an hour waiting on some business to swing my way, so I'll be very grateful to do that for you. Are you going to need some transportation while you're here or are you going to have some family taking you places?"

Treasure thought about his question. "Yea. I'll need some transportation. Give me your info and I'll call you when I need you."

The driver handed her a business card and drove through some back streets on his way to Macon road. "Where are you going on Macon road?" He asked once they arrived.

"This gas station is fine."

David Weaver

She paid the driver the exact amount that she read off of the meter. She didn't want to give him too much and have him getting suspicious, which is what she would have done in the past. She waited until he left, and walked up the street to the Best Western hotel. She saw a black man sitting in his car smoking a blunt when she approached and was so thankful for small blessings.

"Excuse me." She said cautiously. She didn't want to frighten him because she needed him.

"What's up shawty?" He said as he mashed his blunt out in the ash tray.

She cringed upon hearing the word *shawty,* but continued to speak anyways. "Yea let me pay you $100 to get a room in your name for the week."

"Shid shawty, you ain't said nun' for real for real! I'll be right out!"

She gave him the money and waited on him to come out. He walked up to her and handed her the paper packet with the hotel key inside of it.

"Shawty you must not be from here?"

"Nah, I'm not." She responded.

"Well shiddd, the Dirt Mob throwing a big ass party down the street tonight at Club Sky. Them niggas is balling for real for real. You need to show up and fuck with ya' boy tonight. I ain't gon' be doing shit but chillin myself. Ya' feel me?"

Treasure pulled her pistol out calmly. "What's your name?" She asked him.

"Damnnnn shawty! I don't even give a fuck about the lil' $100. I woulda got the room for free. You don't gotta rob me for the money. It ain't that serious ya' feel me?"

Treasure walked up to him until she was standing directly in his black ass face. "I'm not tryna rob your broke ass. You see... my problem is that I don't trust no motherfuckin' body. If my reflection could move in the mirror without me controlling it, I'd blow the brain pigments straight out of that bitch! I don't trust nobody! Nobody! And you are definitely not the x-factor nigga. I don't trust your ass either. Now hand me my second hotel key before I lay your kidneys out here on the concrete."

"Shawtyyyy! Yo' ass is trippin! I don't got no fuckin hotel key! I gave you the got damn key."

"Naw fuck nigga. Niggas like you like to play *games!* And bitches like me don't like to participate! Ain't no got damned way they gave me a hotel key packet, that came with this much space on the inside unless it has been used already. This shit is brand new! And its space on the inside like a key has been slid out. Where the fuck is my key?" Treasure screamed.

"Shawty! I don't got no key! I swear to God!"

Treasure looked in his eyes and listened to his words but she still didn't believe him. She cocked the pistol and saw his light colored blue jeans suddenly turn dark by his crotch area.

"Aight Shawty but please don't kill me! I don't even know why I kept a key for real for real! I swear I'm sorry shawty! Please don't kill me!" He screamed as he handed her the hotel key.

"Get your ass in the car and I better not ever see you again. And I'm talking about ever! I'm putting a bullet in your ass on sight. No clubbing tonight for you nigga. Sit yo' ass home and dream about that shit."

She stood there and watched as he got in his car and peeled off of the premises.

Then she almost kicked herself. Damn I was supposed to kill that nigga. He knows where I stay at now. Damn!

———————

Catfish's friend in Mexico was able to fly him into Columbus GA's private airport. "Man I don't know about this Amigo."

"But I make this flight twice per week. It's safe I promise you. Security is almost non-existent my brother. You will be just fine. They let me fly in as if I was just flying from the next city. Everybody knows that if it wasn't for Columbus GA's private airport, then the drug game in the entire state of Georgia would suffer. It's only so much you can bring in with vehicles without getting caught. Relax brother."

Catfish was surprised at how effortless the flight from Mexico to Columbus was. He called his contact as soon as he left out of the small airport. "Well, I'm already in Columbus, so where do I go to meet the lady who needs help?"

"Treasure. She called earlier and said that she was staying at the Best Western. She also said she got the room in somebody else's name so I don't know how secure that is."

Catfish wrote down the information and went to call a taxi.

———————

When Catfish's taxi was arriving, his cab driver waved at another taxi driver who was leaving out. He glanced into the back seat of the cab and made eye contact with one of the most beautiful women he had ever seen in his entire life. *Treasure,* he thought as he felt his heart beat speed up to triple its normal rate. "Hey, can you ask that cab driver where they're headed?" Catfish asked.

The cab driver turned and smiled at him. "My man! She was beautiful right?"

Catfish blushed as he sat there and waited on the information. It had been so long since he'd felt that way about a woman that he didn't know how to act. The last time his heart skipped a beat for a woman, he ended up marrying her. He didn't even know Treasure good enough to be thinking like that, but just having the idea of it sure made him feel good.

His cab driver picked up the radio and tapped a button. "Hey, where you headed Bronzin?"

There was static on the radio, and then a reply. "Right down the street to Club Sky. What's up?"

"I was just wondering. I'll holla at you later on. I have a few things to do." He placed the radio receiver down and turned to face his passenger. "Is that where you wanna' go? Club Sky? It's not far from here at all."

"How far is not far?" Catfish asked.

"I mean… you can actually walk down there. It's like a few blocks down the street."

"Uhm… I'll call you if I need you. Here's $300. I need you to be there when I need you. Dead serious!" Catfish handed him the money and stared him in the eyes menacingly. The driver knew that if he accepted the money, then he would need to do exactly as Catfish asked him. He wanted to turn the money

David Weaver

down but he knew how bad his family needed the financial help. $300 was more than he made on most entire days, so it was nothing to be on call for the rest of the night for his passenger.

"Yes sir. I'll just stick to this area for the rest of the night. If you need me, just ring me."

Catfish got out of the car with only one bag in his hand. In the bag he had a sawed off shotgun, an entire case of shells, and a new pack of tank tops. He didn't come to Columbus for a vacation, so it pissed him off that Treasure was going clubbing when she was on the run. He thought about calling his amigo friend and setting up his return trip to the Philippines, but since he was already there…

He was headed to the front desk when he saw a few things that looked out of place. There was a car sitting outside of the hotel with its lights off and two people sitting inside of it. One person had a radio in his hand and the other person had binoculars on his face. He was aiming the binoculars on a room, and from just a glance Catfish knew that they had to be looking for Treasure.

Another unmarked vehicle drove into the parking lot and parked a couple parking spaces down from the other car. A police car drove up to the restaurant across from the hotel and parked. He got out of the car and waved at the unmarked cars down the way. The passengers waved back.

Another unmarked car pulled in and stopped at the front entrance. For a moment Catfish thought the unmarked car was coming for him. For a second he thought that he'd been set-up by the taxi driver or his amigo friend.

But neither of them were the case. The undercover detective walked straight past him and went to the front desk of the hotel. He knew he needed to get to the club immediately so that he could warn Treasure of the sting operation that was about to go down. He turned away from the hotel and started walking towards where the driver told him the club was supposed to be.

Treasure was dressed to kill.

She had on a black dress and black lipstick. She had a black handbag and a black handgun was inside of her purse. She had on black heels and black earrings. If she never got a chance to do anything else in life, she wanted to make sure that she did 5 in for setting her up. There was no way she was going to let that nigga live. She was going to make sure that he died that night.

She paid the security extra money just to walk straight through. When she got to the metal detector, she paid the security $1,000 each to let her walk straight through without being checked. Once she got inside of the packed club, she looked around the room slowly.

It was so smoke filled that she couldn't tell who was who. She moved around the crowd as best as she could. She tried to ignore the men who kept touching her on her butt and continued trying to get herself in a better position. She saw a crowd of men standing in the VIP area, and thought for sure that that's where she would find the man who betrayed her. She walked closer to the stage and out of nowhere, a fist clobbered her straight across the face.

"Bitch is you looking for me?" 5 said as he punched her in the face again. The rest of the Dirt Mob stood behind 5 as he stood in Treasure's face. "I knew you was coming back to try to find me bitch!

You thought you could pay security to bring a fucking gun in *my club* and get away with it? Bitch you dead for trying to kill me!"

He punched her in the face again, causing her to hit the ground like a lifeless doll. A tall guy with huge arms walked up to 5 and put his hands on his shoulder. "That's a woman you're beating on my guy. Leave her alone."

"Mind your own fucking business nigga!" 5 spat as he ignored the man.

The tall man felt anger surge through him and cocked back his fist so that he could hit 5 in the face, but it was too late. Everybody from the dirt mob pulled a pistol out and pointed it at the tall guy.

"What you don't seem to understand is that this is my club fuck nigga! Now get yo' bitch ass out of here before you get shot!" 5 screamed.

Treasure tried to stand up and 5 kicked her back down to the ground like she was a grown man.

"I'ma kill you bitch! That's on everything!"

Catfish saw a crowd of black people running out of the club by the time he arrived. He scanned the crowd looking to see if he could spot Treasure or not. When he didn't see her, he walked into the club when everyone was trying to get out. A few people bumped into him on accident, but they bounced off of him.

"That nigga beating that poor girl up!" A girl screamed as she passed by him.

Quickly he opened his bag and pulled out his shotgun. Deep in his heart he knew that Treasure was in some form of trouble, but when he saw Malcolm's snitch ass brother in the club; he knew exactly what it was. "Fuckkkkkk nigga!" Catfish bellowed as he pointed the shotgun at 5. "Nigga do you know how many years I been looking to fuck you up?"

KA-BOOM!

Catfish shot his gun into the ceiling and made everybody get on the floor. "Drop your guns or these buck shots will tear your ass up little boys!"

The Dirt Mob instantly knew who Catfish was when they saw him. They knew that any member of the Bankroll Squad had to be respected by street law.

No matter how arrogant they wanted to be and no matter how big and bad they wanted to seem, they knew they didn't want problems with anyone from the Bankroll Squad. They dropped their pistols on the ground in front of them.

"You got it homey!" 5 said as he knelt down to the ground with the rest of his gang.

Treasure's face was bleeding and she was scared that someone was going to shoot her. She had robbed and shot so many people that there was no telling who it was after her. She closed her eyes as she awaited her fate.

"Treasure! On your feet!" Catfish screamed across the club.

She hurriedly got up and held her palms up facing Catfish. She was shaking from the kick in the stomach and the sound of the explosive gunshot. "Please don't kill me." She pleaded.

Catfish's heart warmed momentarily. "I didn't come to kill you. You asked for help and I'm here. Let's go."

Treasure hurriedly walked across the dance floor and stood beside Catfish. His shotgun was still trained on the Dirt Mob the entire time. "Do you want me to kill them or what?" He asked Treasure.

Treasure looked into 5 eyes and realized that even though he had betrayed her, she still couldn't bring herself to have him killed. She had killed him a million times in her head, and now that he was in her face; she just couldn't have her vision executed. "Let's go. Fuck that nigga."

She walked out of the club and Catfish sneered at the Dirt Mob. "I asked her if she wanted me to kill you and she said no. But she didn't ask me what I wanted to do!"

He cocked the shotgun.

KA-BOOM!

The shell casing flew to the ground and the buck shots separated his knee cap from his thigh. 5 grabbed at his leg as blood drained out of his body like the toilet was overflowing. "Arrrrgghhh shitttttt!"

The rest of the Dirt Mob placed their faces in their hands when they saw the horrible and disgusting gunshot wound. Catfish wanted to go ahead and kill him, but he knew that no matter what, 5 was still

Malcolm's blood brother. No matter how much Malcolm didn't care about 5, he had to still respect the fact that family was family. Especially being that his family was so small. He exhaled and left out of the club.

He walked outside and a crowd of people was standing around staring at the entrance of the door. When they saw the sawed off shotgun in his hand, a lot of people jumped in their cars and took off. He grabbed Treasure's arm gently and looked into her eyes. "Are you ok baby?"

Baby? Treasure thought as she stared back at him. "I'm fine. Thank you." *But how the fuck are you going to call me baby when you don't know me?* She wanted to ask him. But she had seen him in action and knew not to ask a question of that caliber. She followed him as they walked across the club parking lot until they got to the road. She stopped walking at the road.

"Thank you... uhm..."

"Catfish is my name."

"Ok thank you Catfish. However, I don't need your help beyond this point. I'll be fine on my own."

Catfish looked at her with a confused look on his face. "But you needed someone in the Bankroll Squad to assist you. Now that I've traveled from overseas to help you, you don't need help anymore?"

Treasure placed her hand on top of her head and closed her eyes. She opened them and shook her head frantically. Tears came out as she attempted to speak. "Look! I don't know what I want at this point! I don't know if I want to live or die. I'm so lost that I don't even remember if I have ever served a purpose on this earth."

Catfish felt her pain because he felt the same exact way on many nights and days. He swallowed involuntarily as he listened to Treasure release her pain. He knew there was a reason that he felt so drawn to coming over and helping her. In a way, she was just like him.

"So where are you going to stay then?" He asked her.

"I have a room up the street. I'm going to go get my stuff and probably switch hotels for the night."

Catfish shook his head. "See, that's why you need me." He said as he walked up to her carefully. "You need someone who can watch your back and wash your back when it was time. You need someone who can think for you and be thankful for you all the time. You need someone who understands you when you can't understand yourself. Someone who you understand when he can't understand his own self. You need a man who won't betray you or replace you Treasure.

You need someone who was built for you and made for your future. A man who can be himself with you, and a man that you can be yourself around. I know what you need Treasure. Although I don't know what you desire or what you want, I promise you I know exactly what you need. You need a man like me in your life. You need a man that you can grow to love and one that will do the same for you.

You can't go back to the hotel Treasure. Police have been setting up to grab you all night long. When I was pulling into the hotel, you were leaving out. Me and you looked each other in the face, but I don't know if you remember. After you left, unmarked police cars were setting up outside of your room. You can not go back if you wanna stay free."

Treasure absorbed the words that Catfish spoke to her. She looked into his eyes and saw something in a man that she had never seen before in her life. *Loyalty. Strength. Power. Honesty. Courage. Protection.*

The eyes didn't lie, and Catfish's eyes felt like he was still speaking the truth to her even when his mouth was closed. She was quickly becoming captivated by the powerful gentleman standing before her, but she still had a bit of skepticism about the situation. She had prayed on many nights for someone like him, and on the night when it seemed as if she was supposed to die; he had come through for her. She felt as if the angels had truly shined favor on her and she was grateful for it.

But she had to be honest.

"I'm a wanted woman Catfish. I'm wanted by the government dead or alive."

Catfish laughed. "Then we're a match made in heaven. I'm wanted by the government dead or alive also. After we escaped the country, I broke *back* into the United States to come help your ass out."

A crowd was staring at them as they exchanged convo, and it started making Treasure nervous. "Let's get out of here Catfish."

"Aight, I got a taxi man waiting on me to call him."

Treasure balked at the suggestion. "A taxi man? That's not how I roll! If you say you understand me, then I need you to understand me for real. Let me see that shotgun!"

She reached for it and grabbed it but Catfish held on to it a little tighter. "I don't know if that would be a good idea Treasure. The kickback from this gun would knock you on your ass. Plus it's a certain way you have to aim it. When you shoot it the buckshots go—"

Treasure snatched the shotgun out of his hand and walked up to a black man sitting on the hood of his Buick Regal. "Ain't you the one that slapped me on the ass?"

"Hell nawl! I ain't slapped shit!" He screamed as he jumped off the hood with his hands held out.

Treasure turned and looked at Catfish. "We got a car right here. Let's go to-"

David Weaver

"Watch out Treasure!"

Before Treasure had time to turn around, the man tried to grab the shotgun out of her hand. She fought back for the weapon and gave him a knee to the nuts in order to keep him at bay. He crouched down in agony, clutching at his private parts in anger.

"Bitch! I'ma kill you if I ever see you again!" He screamed.

KA-BOOM!

Treasure blew a hole in his head so big that she couldn't even remember how his head was supposed to look. He was definitely going to be closed casket material once his mother identified his body. She jumped in the Buick with Catfish and hit the gas.

"Treasure I have somebody at the local airport who is going to let us fly straight to Mexico. No bullshit." Catfish said as Treasure speeded on the expressway.

When she was in the club parking lot she remembered seeing some unmarked cars parked off in the distance, but she figured that they could have been dope boy's cars instead of undercover police. As she drove on the expressway she saw more unmarked cars behind her, trailing her but standing back so not to be noticed.

She exited the expressway abruptly, and when she got to the stoplight she saw another unmarked car exit the expressway also. She drove down the street and made a left turn into a gas station. The car that was following her kept going straight and she sighed.

"Treasure, are you listening to me? I want you in the Philippines with me. I know you don't know me enough to make that decision, but I know you know that you can't just stay in America as one of the most wanted black women to ever exist in the country. Please understand that it's not just America who wants you the most…"

Treasure stopped studying her surroundings and stared into Catfish's honest eyes. His words were touching, but she knew that it would never work. "Who else wants me besides America?"

Catfish grabbed her hand carefully. "I want you."

David Weaver

A tingle shot down Treasure's spine as she heard those words.

"Come to Borocay and be with me Treasure. And if you don't want to be with me, still come to Borocay and be free from the United States. Either way, it's a win-win for you. What do you say?" Catfish said as he admired Treasure's beauty. He was so deeply impressed and intrigued by this woman, so powerfully moved by her that he had no other option but to tell her how he felt.

Treasure looked across the street and saw another unmarked car at the other gas station. Then she saw someone who looked familiar come out of the store and get into the car. They were just sitting there, apparently waiting on her next move. Catfish wasn't paying attention at his surroundings. He was only focused on the woman his spirit had led him to. Even the way her chest moved when she breathed was a turn on for him. He was silently praying that she saw things his way and left for Mexico with him.

Treasure turned to Catfish and smiled. "I like you a lot, but I'm not coming. I truly thank you for feeling how you feel about me, but I don't trust any woman or any man. Please understand my position for what it is as opposed to what it isn't. I'm sure you're a great man, but I am not a great woman."

Catfish stared at her in silence. Immediately he fell back into his protective shell. "No problem Treasure. Well, you want me to call a cab or are you going to drop me off at the—"

"Yea call a cab. Bye Catfish." Treasure said coldly. She didn't mean to be so cold, but it seemed that the more someone liked her, the colder her heart was to them. She simply couldn't allow herself to be bamboozled and tricked again.

Catfish grabbed his bag with the shotgun in it, got out, and slammed the door. He was going to catch the next flight straight back to Mexico. He wanted to be alone in the comforts of his own home. *Fuck the United States. They don't have nothing to offer me anyways.*

———————

Treasure watched as Catfish got into a taxi and took off. She waited until he got far off into the distance and drove the opposite direction. The unmarked cars followed her. She abruptly turned

David Weaver

through a parking lot and they weren't able to adjust appropriately. She looked in her rearview mirror to see if it was indeed the person that she'd recognized. *It was.*

She knew that it would take the unmarked car time to adjust and turn around their car, so she decided to ditch the car she was driving. She saw a guy in the parking lot in a Red Mercedes. He was on the cell phone and bent down wiping his rims and shining his tires. She pulled over beside him and jumped out.

"Get off the phone." Treasure said as she pulled her gun out of her purse. The man ended the call immediately and put his hands up.

"I'm going to pay you. I'm giving you all of the money I got on me. It's about eighty thousand dollars in cash. You take this money and take this car to your house! I promise you that you won't get in trouble. It's me that they want, not you. Take this money and this car to your house. Later tomorrow morning, I want you to go to the Best Western on Macon road and use this key." She said as she handed him the key and a stack of money.

"I left a bag in there with about $300,000 worth of drugs and money combined. I'm giving it to you in exchange for this car and a future favor if I ever need you. Deal?"

"Hell yea that's a deal!"

"Oh yea. And swap phones with me."

They swapped phones and cars, and both went in their separate directions.

Catfish was at a bar in Mexico relaxing. He knew that it was risky to have flown into the United States, but it pissed him off that he had done it for nothing at all. He felt like there was a great chemistry between him and Treasure, but apparently she felt otherwise. He enjoyed the excitement and adrenaline rush of drama, and nothing seemed to put him in a more jovial mood than pure negative mischief.

His amigo friend came to the bar and sat beside him. "You alright Catfish?" He asked him with a concerned look on his face.

David Weaver

Catfish nodded his head. "I'm fine." He lied. He glanced at the wedding ring on his friend's hand and looked down at his bare fist. He glanced up at the television and saw that there was breaking news going on in Georgia. He wasn't fluent in Spanish so he couldn't make out what they were saying.

"Migo, what are they saying?" He asked quickly.

His amigo listened and translated slowly. "Says they... have had Treasure's place surrounded since 6 hours ago... says they know for a fact she's in the house... says they are going to raid the location... says they tracked her and.... Say they're going to take her into custody dead or alive... says..."

"Catfish you don't need a translator baby." Treasure said as she sat right beside him at the bar.

Catfish's eyes lit up when he saw her. "Treasure! But- but- what they talking about on the news?" He said as he stared transfixed at Treasure's creation.

"They were tracking that phone that I bought from the homeless bitch in Atlanta GA. That's how they kept tabs on me the whole time. Shit was real crazy though. I switched phones and cars with this dude, and I told his ass to drive fast and don't stop or come out of his house for nobody. I gave him all the money I had except the money it took for me to fly, so I'm broke as a joke." She said with a solemn look on her face.

Catfish frowned. "But how did you fly over here? My friend only makes that flight twice per week. Who flew you?" He asked skeptically. For a minute he thought she was on some set up shit, but that quickly dissolved when he heard her answer.

"Man Catfish, I was sitting directly behind you on the entire flight. I listened to you talk to yourself and call me all kinds of bitches and hoes, sluts and dummies. The way you talked about me on that flight let me know that you were truly into me. At first I was just going to just do as you say... just come to the Philippines to be free from the United States, but after listening to your passion about me on the flight let me know that there is no place in the world that I would rather be than in your arms.

"Don't think after hearing you call me all of those names that I didn't have it in my right mind to just blow your brains out the first chance I got! But I also knew that when it came to dealing with someone who really cared about you, that a lady such as myself

David Weaver

would rather be in your arms as opposed to being armed. Catfish I'm here. I wanna get to know you better. I wanna see what we can grow by planting this seed of trust."

The amigo smiled and patted Catfish on the back. "This woman is for you my man. I almost didn't let her make the trip until she explained herself to me. This lady was specifically designed to be a perfect match to a man like yourself. Congratulations!"

Catfish watched as his amigo walked away.

He turned back to Treasure and smiled. "But what about the Lipstick Clique gang that you were running? What are you going to do about that?"

She shook her head. "I realized that you can't build loyalty, a person has to already have it. And when other loyal people combine, it only strengthens loyalty. I am the Lipstick Clique. Period. I'm the entire organization all packaged into one person. But I've been focusing more on Treasure as the woman instead of Treasure as the Lipstick Clique. And Treasure as the woman, has finally been blessed to her treasure, as a man."

Catfish stood up and helped her off of the stool. When she got down, he wrapped his arms around her snugly. Both of them closed their eyes and enjoyed the fragrance of promise. They absorbed passion and excitement, and it electrified both of them greatly.

Catfish's amigo friend watched from the entrance of the bar and smiled. He knew that they were going to be together for a very long time. It wasn't too often that two people connected and displayed such an intense level of attraction, but it was evident to him and for all onlookers.

Congratulations my amigos. He exited the bar.

---

18 Months Later

The federal agent walked back and forth in the conference room as the U.S. Marshalls escorted the last person to their seat. The agent glanced at the crowd and took a deep breath. He picked up a piece of chalk and walked to the board. On it he wrote: TARGET: BANKROLL SQUAD.

"As you all know, most of you will never be going home. Ever! Many of you have double life sentences and some of you are getting ready to receive death penalty sentences. So what this means is that many of you are going to die in prison. You will never see the outside of the prison walls again.

Many of you have been friends with people in either the Lipstick Click or the Bankroll Squad organization, and many of you still remain friends with very prominent members. What I'm about to tell you is no joke. It's simple and straight to the point. We need assistance with this. We need the Bankroll Squad organization shut down completely and all of its members in custody.

If you all help us with this, you will get an opportunity to get back out on the streets to do so. We've made deals with people previously, but my director simply believes that we had the wrong people in those positions. Today we believe we have the right group of people for the job. I'm about to pass around a sheet of paper. I'm going to give you all ten minutes to decide.

Sign your name on the paper if you're going to help us bring the squad down once and for all. If you're not going to help, you will be placed in the hole and will not be allowed any communication with anyone for the remainder of this investigation."

The federal agent dropped the paper on the table and a pen and walked out.

Ten minutes later, he walked back in and picked up the paper. He smiled when he saw the results of his speech. Everyone had signed the paper. He smiled at the crowd and motioned for his partner to take over with further directions. He walked out of the room staring at the paper in disbelief.

The director was outside of the room waiting. "Who signed it? Anyone?"

"Everybody signed it. Everyone is going to help bring the squad down."

"Salisha? Nerow? 5? Them three plus the others?"

"Yes!" He said enthusiastically. "All of them!"

"What about Malcolm Powers? Did he really sign that paper to be a snitch?"

David Weaver

The federal agent held up the sheet of paper for the director to see.

AUTHOR'S NOTES

Hello, I'm David Weaver; 30-year-old owner of SBR Publications and author of the bestselling Bankroll Squad series plus many more. If you would like to keep in contact with me, there's my InstaGram: @bankrollsquad which is the same as my Twitter: @bankrollsquad and it's Malcolm Powers Bawss on Facebook.

Writing this was crazy difficult because it had to take place before and after "The Power Family" book at the same damn time. So in essence, you would have to read "The Power Family" first, so you could understand what went on before and after it. Pause, let me think about that. Ok, that's right.

The ending of this story will be continued in "Bankroll Squad 4," which is set to be released on October 29th, 2013. It is the main event. I seriously suggest that you pre-order it on Kindle so that it can be wirelessly delivered to you at midnight. Click Here to Pre-Order Bankroll Squad 4

David Weaver

As always, I appreciate my supporters from the bottom of my heart. I am thankful for each person who read and discuss books by David Weaver. Thank you so much!

My website will be up shortly, and you will be able to order my Luxury Water or items my Luxury clothing line. It will be www.DAVIDLUXURY.com

□-If it's not up by the time you're done reading this, check back in a few days. Thank you! #TBRS = TeamBankRollSquad and yes I have my tattoo. □